WIRED COURAGE

PARADISE CRIME THRILLERS BOOK 9

TOBY NEAL

Cover Design: Jun Ares aresjun@gmail.com

Formatting: Jamie Davis

"Being deeply loved by someone gives you strength, while loving someone deeply gives you courage."
~Lao Tzu

CHAPTER ONE

Day One

DISCIPLINE WAS BEAUTIFUL, even when it hurt.

Pim Wat stood on the stone balcony of the temple overlooking the courtyard. Rows of acolytes, dressed identically in black cotton *gi,* practiced before their master. The crisp movements of the closely-guarded martial arts routine were already embedded in her own muscle memory, and if she'd joined the young men and women in their tidy rows, she could have performed their routine perfectly, too.

Someone missed a movement, the mistake glaring in the crisp rows of conformity, and the Master raised his baton.

All movement ceased. The rows of recruits froze into stillness. The Master lowered the baton, and the recruits dropped to the ground to do push-ups.

They would do push-ups until he raised the baton again.

Armita appeared at Pim Wat's elbow. "Your tea, mistress."

Pim Wat took the hand-thrown porcelain teacup without looking at her maid. She sniffed the jasmine-scented brew, then took a sip. Scalding hot, just as she preferred. "Acceptable."

She seated herself on one of two chunks of amethyst that had

1

been beveled into stools. A large tiger's-eye plinth, glowing with bronze iridescence, served as a table. Armita faded back into the building after leaving a lacquered tray holding a pot and another teacup.

Perhaps the Master would join Pim Wat, but he didn't always. She willed him to, craving the drug of his presence.

The recruits were still doing push-ups. At last the Master raised his baton, and they leapt to their feet in one accord. He barked out an order, and the routine began again. He tapped a student on the end of one of the rows with the baton, handing it over. The black-clad young man took the carved ivory cane reverently, and stepped into the leader's place in front.

The Master strode toward Pim Wat, and she smiled with satisfaction as he glanced up at her.

Moments later he seated himself on the other chunk of amethyst and picked up his teacup. He closed his eyes to savor the tea, some of the most expensive and exquisite in the world. Pim Wat feasted her hungry gaze on the man that she loved with an unseemly and obsessive passion.

The Master looked no more than thirty, though he was at least Pim Wat's age. Long black hair, braided and decorated with carved jade, hung down his muscled back. The smooth fans of his lashes rested against golden-skinned, high cheekbones, contrasting with straight dark brows. He opened deep purple eyes that must be the result of some multi-racial encounter of ancestors. "When is she coming to us?"

Pim Wat tightened her mouth in annoyance and hid her expression behind the delicate, hand-thrown cup. "My daughter is stubborn. I've told you this."

"The Yām Khûmkạn requires her."

"And I've told you that she cannot be persuaded. Especially now that she's pregnant." Pim Wat's cup rattled as she set it on the tray. *She was going to be a grandmother.* What a reminder that time was passing—despite all her efforts, she was getting old. "I have tried everything to get her to come, even threats. She has refused."

"Does she suspect anything about what we really want?"

"No. How could she? But she does not trust me." Pim Wat made a fist. "I cannot command her like I used to."

"You must manage your emotions, Beautiful One." The Master leaned toward her, but instead of a kiss, he drew a line down her profile with a finger and tipped up her chin. He rolled the ball of his thumb across her lower lip. Pim Wat's eyes fluttered closed in anticipation and her body trembled. "Take her, if there is no other way. Do what you must do."

His touch disappeared.

Pim Wat kept her eyes closed for a long moment, still hoping, but when she opened them, he was gone.

"Manage my emotions, by Quan Yin's left tit," she snarled. "Armita! My tea is cold!"

Armita came out onto the balcony and whisked away the tea. Pim Wat looked down at the practice area, but it no longer entertained her. She followed her maid into the main chamber of her apartment.

Thick, luxurious carpets and rich silk drapes softened the harsh stone walls and floors of the ancient room. "We must prepare a plan to get Sophie Malee," Pim Wat said.

Armita's eyes flashed, just a tiny flare of defiance. "Are you sure that's a good idea, mistress? She is well protected."

"The Master wants her, and thus she will come. Once she's here, they won't be able to take her back. The stronghold of the Yām Khûmkạn is too remote and fortified." Pim Wat turned toward a tall, exotic wood armoire. "Back to Hawaii I must go. Such a long, tiresome flight." Pim Wat pinched the back of Armita's arm viciously as the maid reached out to open the armoire. "And that's for questioning me."

3

CHAPTER TWO

Day Seven

"Where's the baby?"

Sophie woke to a gentle shake on her shoulder, a whispered question in her ear. She opened gummy eyes and sat up, her hand falling to her belly—a flat, empty belly, deflated as a balloon with the air let out. She glanced at the empty bassinet beside the bed, then up into the warm brown eyes of her child's father. "Jake must have her."

Alika squeezed her shoulder. "I'll go check. Get some rest while you can."

Sophie slid back down, her cheek finding the soft pillow as her heavy eyes fell shut.

Her whole body felt like it had been pummeled with rubber hammers. The midwife said it had been a textbook delivery, but that didn't mean it hadn't been eighteen hours of hard labor that made going ten rounds in a mixed martial arts ring seem lightweight.

Momi Tasanee Wolcott Smithson had been born twelve hours before, two weeks premature but a healthy length and weight. Sophie smiled even as she drifted off, picturing her daughter's full head of curly black hair, her velvety skin, her tiny fingers and toes with their shell-like nails. Nothing her mother had been through during her pregnancy appeared to have marred Momi's perfection; the baby was rightly named "pearl" in Hawaiian.

Such a relief. Sophie had never stopped worrying about that ugly first trimester.

Sophie startled awake as the door opened again. She sat up.

Alika and her boyfriend Jake both stood in the doorway, and they both wore identical worried expressions. Sophie's breasts ached with fullness. "Where's Momi? I can tell she needs to be fed."

Jake cleared his throat, advancing into the room to sit on the bed beside Sophie. He slid a hand over her shoulder and drew her close, kissing the top of her head. She leaned into him, and his thickly muscled arm tightened around her.

She smelled an acrid tang on him—*fear.*

"We can't find her," Alika said. "We've checked the house." He advanced into the room and opened the closet, the bureau, searching restlessly as if he couldn't stop himself, his big body vibrating with tension.

Alarm flushed through Sophie like a blast of arctic air. She wrenched away from Jake. "What do you mean, she's gone? I nursed Momi and put her to bed beside me in the bassinet. Jake, you saw me do that. One of you must have picked her up! There's no one else in the house, right?"

"No one that we know of," Jake pushed a hand through military-short dark hair, his eyes the color of ash.

Alika lifted the skirt of the bed to peer underneath. "I don't know what could have happened. Where could she be?"

"What, you think I hid her under the bed?" Sophie's voice had risen. "This isn't happening." She surged out of bed. "There has to be an explanation. I'll find her . . ."

Sophie was out of the bedroom and running, heedless of pain, of dizziness, of the heavy aching of her breasts as she tore through the upstairs bedrooms of Alika's showplace of a home, where she'd been ensconced since she'd arrived a week before. Jake tried to calm her and support her, but Sophie batted him aside as she clung to the railing and hurried down the main staircase into the great room of Alika's mansion.

Sophie checked the living room, the kitchen, the downstairs guest room, the bathroom, the office. Her and Jake's dogs, Tank and Ginger, nudged and chased her, sensing her distress as she frantically looked for the baby.

"Momi!" Sophie cried. "Momi!"

The baby couldn't answer. She knew that. She knew it! But Momi was gone! It was impossible but true. Who had taken her? How? Why?

Sophie's body felt disconnected from her churning mind and flaring emotions—a painful, irrelevant meat-bag that no longer held her precious daughter.

When she'd searched the whole place, run around the grounds and through the four-car garage, Sophie collapsed on the bluestone steps of the mansion, staring up at a deep blue sky filled with Kaua`i's high white cumulus clouds.

The dogs crowded close, licking whatever bit of bare skin they could reach. Sophie wrapped one arm over her eyes to shut out the light, and the other over her hard, full breasts, feeling wetness saturate the soft fabric of her shirt as her milk let down.

She heard a keening sound off in the distance.

She was the one making that strange cry.

Arms, the heat of a human body, motion, soothing sounds. Jake picked Sophie up and carried her inside. He took her into the downstairs guest room and shut the door. He settled her in his lap on the bed and rocked her as if she were the child, murmuring into her hair, stroking her back. "It will be okay. We'll find her. She's going to be fine."

His mantra helped shut out the terror, the blackness of an unspeakable loss. Sophie closed her eyes and clung to him, breathing in his familiar scent, comforting even when bitter with stress. "She needs me, Jake. And I need her."

"I know, honey. I know."

Outside the bedroom, voices—Alika on the phone, then talking to his grandmother, then both of them making calls. The bustle of other humans, searching for her daughter.

Time passed.

Jake whispered in her ear, his arms and body heat surrounding her, warming her. "Did you see anything? Hear anything?"

"No!"

"Could you have . . . sleepwalked? Put her somewhere?"

Sophie recoiled. "No! Of course not! You saw what I saw. Momi is gone! I don't know how, but she is gone!" She clawed her way out of his arms. *That he'd even imagined she had done something with Momi . . .*

Sirens. The slam of doors. The dogs barking. More murmuring voices. Thump of feet on the stairs.

The investigators would be checking her room, looking for clues, a ransom note—but there was nothing.

Her baby was just gone, as if she'd never been there at all.

CHAPTER THREE

Day Eight

CONNOR, aka Sheldon Hamilton, Sophie and Jake's boss at their private security firm, waited impatiently as his driver Thom Tang parked a Security Solutions SUV behind the police vehicles jamming up the driveway at Alika Wolcott's Princeville home. He got out of the vehicle and looked back at Thom. "Make sure both the helicopter and the jet are tuned up and fully fueled. We may be leaving soon."

"You got it, boss." The Thai man inclined his head. "I'll call the fuel company right now."

Connor navigated around three cop cars parked willy-nilly, blocking the driveway. He'd taken the jet from his private island in Thailand as soon as he heard Sophie had delivered the baby early; he'd landed on Kaua'i only to learn that the infant had been kidnapped.

He couldn't imagine what Sophie, Jake, and Alika were going through when his own shock and fury were so acute—and he hadn't even met the baby they'd all been looking forward to for so many long months.

Esther Ka`awai, Alika's grandmother, let him into the mansion. The Hawaiian woman's face was haggard, her black and silver hair straggling out of a knot at the back of her neck. "Oh good, Mr. Hamilton, you're here. Jake and Sophie will be so glad to see you, and have Security Solutions help with all of this." Esther leaned in close, cupping her mouth to whisper in his ear. "The police are acting like Sophie did something to the baby."

"What?" Connor recoiled. "Obviously this was the work of someone who wishes her harm, and there's nothing that would hurt her more than losing her child."

"I know." Esther smoothed her flowered muumuu housedress with gnarled hands. Her large brown eyes were shadowed, but calm. "I'm glad I told you this, then. The longer there is no ransom note, the more Jake and Alika begin to believe it, as well as the police. Such a thing is like poison in a wound—it enters in small amounts, and spreads to kill."

Connor stared at the dignified older woman in growing horror. "This will destroy Sophie. I have to get her out of here."

"You may not be able to," Esther said, but she was speaking to his back as Connor strode out of the foyer, heading for the mansion's great room.

Jake, Alika, and several uniformed police officers sat on couches facing each other, with a phone in the middle of the coffee table. Connor swept the room with a glance, taking in coffee cups and a plate of malasadas.

A young blond detective approached him, holding up a badge that identified him as Jack Jenkins. "And you are?"

"Sheldon Hamilton. CEO of Security Solutions, Jake Dunn and Sophie Smithson's employer." He pinned Jake with a glare. "Where's Sophie? Why aren't you taking care of her?"

"She's sleeping. Sedated," Jake said. The ex-Special Forces operative looked pale and somehow diminished. "We couldn't calm her down. She went a little nuts."

Alika stood up. He, too, looked exhausted and wan. "We tried everything to get her to settle, but after the police tried to interview her, she went a little berserk." An amputee, he gestured with his remaining arm to a sideboard covered with smashed crockery and an overturned sculpture.

Connor cursed. "Of course she did! Where is she?" He spun on a heel, looking toward the stairs.

All of the officers stood up and their hands dropped to their weapons. "Stay where you are, sir," Detective Jenkins said. "This is an active investigation. If you have any information pertinent to the case, we need your full cooperation."

Connor ignored the man, returning his attention to Jake. "Why haven't you called Sophie's friend Marcella Scott at the FBI? Or her father Frank Smithson, the ambassador?"

Jake cleared his throat. "We have confidence in our team here," he said. His eyes darted to the side, signaling something. He did it again, and Connor spotted a small black device on the small side table—*all of this was being recorded.*

What could he say to get the police looking in a different direction than Sophie for the baby's disappearance?

"I'd like to get your statement, sir," the detective said. "Come into the dining area with me."

The baby's disappearance had to have something to do with Sophie's terrible mother, Pim Wat, with her ties to Thailand's version of the CIA. Jake, at least, had to suspect that too, even if Alika didn't know enough to point a finger in that direction. But these local cops would never believe some far-fetched tale about Sophie's spy assassin mother without some kind of evidence.

Connor narrowed his eyes at Jake. "When Sophie wakes, tell her I'm here. That I'm very concerned about how her *mother* will react to this news." Jake's shock-dulled eyes opened wider—he got the message. "Also, I want you and Thom to do a foot-by-foot grid sweep of the grounds outside the house. Look for any marks of footprints or a vehicle. The ground is soft from rain—there might be something outside that you missed."

"Excuse me, Mr. Hamilton. We are in charge of this investigation," Detective Jenkins said. "Who do you think you are, coming in here and telling everyone what to do?"

"I'm the CEO of a multi-million-dollar security company that specializes in private kidnap rescue, and two of my best operatives were just hit with a crime we deal with every day." His eyes felt hot as his gaze clashed with the detective's. "What I can't understand is a roomful of cops sitting around on their butts, drinking coffee and eating donuts, when a newborn infant has been snatched—and close to both a road and a cliff for easy getaway by car or air. No wonder Ms. Smithson is so upset."

"The Kaua`i Police Department is in charge of this case. Are you going to cooperate, sir, or do I need to cuff you and take you in officially?" Jenkins wasn't backing down.

They stared at each other another long minute.

"I'll cooperate," Connor said. He turned to glare at Jake, again. "Do what I said, or you're fired."

The detective thrust Connor inside the downstairs office leading off the great room, and slammed the door. Connor walked across the graciously appointed space and sat in a chair beside Alika Wolcott's desk, a drafting table covered in architectural plans. "Get your cops outside, searching. Time is of the essence in a case like this."

"Let's just put the brakes on for a minute, here, Mr. Hamilton." Jenkins pulled a rolling office chair away from the drafting table and sat facing Connor. He took out a tablet and a stylus. "Give me some background on yourself."

"Not until you authorize a grid search of the grounds," Connor said. "Every minute we sit here wagging our jaws, the perps get farther away with a tiny infant who needs her mother. Yes, I have information germane to this investigation, but I'm not giving it to you without some hope of finding evidence to back it up."

Jenkins had intelligent blue eyes, currently narrowed in frustration. "See this from our point of view. We get a call that a newborn baby's missing. There's no ransom note or phone call since the disappearance. No one has seen or heard anything. The last person to interact with the infant is the child's mother, a woman with a mental health history who killed her ex-husband and has just given birth to an illegitimate child she may or may not want."

The description was chilling, and infuriating in its surface accuracy.

"Rather than looking for clues as to who snatched the baby, you must have just been talking to a few people." Connor folded his arms over his chest. "And you haven't done much homework if that's who you think Sophie is. But I'll cut you some slack if you authorize that search. Your men are just sitting there. What can it hurt?" Someone had thrown Sophie under the bus, exposing her history. Who could it have been?

Jenkins took a long moment to lock eyes with Connor in a stare down before taking his walkie off his belt and barking orders into it. "And have the boyfriend and baby's father help search, too. We can use the manpower with the amount of ground we have to cover." Jenkins hung the walkie back on his belt. "Satisfied?"

"For the time being. Who did you interview so far?" He wanted the name of whomever had sold Sophie out, and he didn't think it was Jake, Alika, or Alika's formidable but loving grandma.

"I made a few calls before I got here, checking out her background," Jenkins said evasively. "I know a few cops in Honolulu."

Connor's neck flushed. "Well, then, you can also take a little time to look up the Security Solutions website. Search my operative Sophie Smithson's credentials. Check out her background in the FBI and her skills in computers and security. Look up Jake Dunn as well and check out his decorated past as a Special Forces commando. And read over my bio while you're at it. That should bring you up to speed on who we really are." Connor took out his tablet. "After that, I think we can have a more intelligent discussion."

Jenkins tightened his mouth and waited a long beat, but when it was clear Connor wasn't going to engage any further, he got out his smartphone and worked it with his thumbs.

Connor scrolled through his feeds. He highlighted several websites and articles as Jenkins perused the Security Solutions website. "Do you have an email address? I have some background information for you and your team to take a look at."

Jenkins was impressed by what he had been reading so far because the man's tone had changed as he rattled off the email address.

Connor shunted background he had gathered on Pim Wat to Jenkins. He had been studying Sophie's elusive mother for a while now, and he'd prepared a file on her in case he should ever need to share it with some government agency or law enforcement. The international spy and assassin kept a low profile, posing as an intellectual socialite who supported obscure art and charity causes around the world. *If ever the time had come to out Pim Wat to the cops, it was now.*

"Okay, Mr. Hamilton." The detective looked up from his phone at Connor. "I get it that you're the billionaire genius CEO of a corporation that specializes in artificial intelligence home security systems, kidnap rescue, and private mercenaries." He blew out an annoyed breath. "That doesn't mean you get to take over this investigation and give orders to the Kaua`i Police Department. Let's work together on this."

"That's exactly what I was hoping you'd say." Connor exercised practiced charm as he smiled. "We are a close-knit group. The stress of this situation has gotten us off on the wrong foot. I just want to make sure that you have all the background you need to develop a fully informed investigation. Because the minute I heard the baby had disappeared, I guessed who might have taken her—Pim Wat, Sophie's mother." Connor swiveled the tablet to show a photo of the woman, dressed in a stunning evening gown and shaking the hand of Thailand's prime minister. "There's an open CIA investigation into this woman. Pim Wat is a member of the royal family in Thailand, and she married Sophie's father, ambassador Frank Smithson, in order to gather intel on the United States. She's an operative of a group called the Yām Khûmkạn." Connor leaned forward, giving Jenkins good eye contact. "My theory is that Pim Wat took the baby as a way to gain leverage over Sophie. She has been trying to get Sophie to come to Thailand and get involved with her spy organization. It's kidnapping, but there will be a different kind of demand than usual."

"Wow, that's some deep shit. Do you have any evidence at all of this theory?" Jenkins's brows had risen.

"Trust me. This isn't most cases. This one is way over your pay grade." Connor rolled his shoulders in irritation. "I suggest you focus on how you can support me and my team, rather than muddying the waters by accusing one of my best operatives of doing away with her infant."

Connor might have gone too far in asserting dominance, because Jenkins scowled and reached over to snatch the tablet out of his hands. "I think I will be taking this tablet into evidence. I need some corroboration of these wild-ass things you're saying."

"You'll need a warrant, not to mention a ten-point encryption code to get into it. Good luck with that." Connor stood up, heat and agitation bringing him to his feet. "What happened to 'let's work together on this'?"

Jenkins's phone rang. He took a look at the number, frowned, and then stood up to answer it, walking to the other side of the room and turning his back as if that kept Connor from hearing every word. "Lei, this isn't a good time. Yeah, I've got a kidnapping case here in Princeville . . . You know these people?" Jenkins swiveled to glare at Connor, and Connor returned his gaze coolly as the detective went on. "Okay. Okay, thanks for the heads-up. I'll keep you posted."

Jenkins ended the call. He walked over to Connor, handing back the tablet. "I just heard from my former partner, Sergeant Lei Texeira on Maui. She called to vouch for her good friend Sophie Smithson, and to ask me to let you guys take the lead on the investigation." The man shook his blond head. "I'm not just handing this off to you with this wild story of international spies. You wait in here. If we find anything on the grounds to indicate that the child was taken by a third party, I will let you know. But for now, make yourself comfortable."

The detective walked out. A moment later, Connor went to work with his tablet.

CHAPTER FOUR

Day Eight

JAKE WALKED a slow grid on the grounds outside the mansion. The house's main windows faced a vista of jutting green mountains, turquoise bay, and the smooth, wide curve of a river below. The grounds ended at a steep, jungled bluff plummeting into the Hanalei Valley, and stands of white-barked Java plum trees edged the property.

Alika's newest development showplace included a guesthouse and was bordered by gracious plantings, clusters of bamboo, and islands of bird of paradise surrounding at least an acre of sweeping lawns. Hanalei Valley ahead of him was a captivating view, but Jake had no interest in any of it.

How had he even begun to suspect Sophie? How could he have even hinted of his darkest worry, let alone pretty much accused her of it? *It would be a miracle if she ever forgave him.* Hamilton sweeping in and throwing his weight around was humiliating, but Jake was grateful for the change of perspective. Their boss clearly suspected Pim Wat, a thought that had flickered through his mind—

but he'd been caught up in reacting to the messages he was getting from the cops.

Jake should have considered Pim Wat more seriously. He knew about the woman's clumsy recruitment attempts, and her very silence in the last months prior to becoming a grandmother was suspect. He'd just been so relieved at her disappearance, and Sophie's resultant reduction in stress, that he had put the woman out of his mind.

Jake scanned the smooth lawn, back and forth, back and forth—as his mind flashed to the many long hours of labor he'd been through with Sophie, sharing every tough and amazing moment with her and the midwife. Alika had joined them once the baby was born to meet his daughter, and it had been a beautiful shared moment among the three of them. A situation that could have been weird had somehow become their new normal.

Sophie had to know Jake loved her more than his own life, that he'd do anything for her and tiny Momi.

She'd forgive him.

Eventually.

He hoped.

Jake followed the officers checking around the windows.

His pulse jumped as he spotted a small, rounded shoe print in the soft soil near one of the windows leading into the office. He glanced inside and met Hamilton's narrowed dark brown eyes behind those hipster glasses. The man was seated in front of Alika's desk, cool as a cucumber, working his tablet. He gave Jake a brief nod, his face expressionless, when Jake pointed to the ground.

Jake yelled for the officer nearest him to come check the impression and look for fingerprints around the edge of the window.

Soon they were taking a cast of the footprint. It was just a partial, almost small enough to be a child's shoe—and not likely to belong to whatever yard service kept the grounds in such immaculate shape.

Jake straightened up from watching the officer pour molding compound into the footprint, to see Alika returning at a run with the officer he'd left with for a longer check around the property's edge.

The two men jogged across the lawn from the scrim of trees that bordered the property.

"We found chopper tracks! There's still fuel residue on the grass, and it looks like several people might have been camping out over there," Alika called.

The officer with Alika ostentatiously ignored both of them and addressed the cop that was dusting for prints around the windowsill. "I radioed Detective Jenkins. Looks like someone was surveilling the house and took off in a chopper from beyond the trees."

Jake pulled Alika out of earshot of the cops now clustered around the window. "You know choppers." Alika owned a Bell Jet Ranger. "What kind of bird do you think it was?"

"Obviously I can't tell the exact model, but the skid indentations were long enough to be a good-sized multi-passenger chopper. And someone was definitely staking us out from the trees."

"I found a partial footprint outside the window, though I doubt we'll be so lucky as to find any fingerprints on the sill. This looks to me like a professional snatch-and-grab. What I can't figure out is why the dogs didn't set off an alarm."

They both turned to eye Ginger the Lab and Tank the pit bull. Both dogs' noses were plastered to the glass slider that led off the dining room as they anxiously watched the activity outside.

"Sophie was napping and we were all in the great room when someone took the baby," Alika said, his eyes closed as he reconstructed the series of events. "The dogs were in the room with us. Tutu had just made us all breakfast, including the dogs. Remember that? We were all on the phone and doing social media posts of the baby." He hunched over suddenly, as if his stomach hurt. "Ah, dammit. Poor Sophie. I feel sick that we thought she might have had anything to do with it."

Jake and Alika had formed an uneasy friendship in the months since finding out that Sophie was pregnant. Confident that Sophie and Alika's romantic interest was over, Jake had come to see that the man had good instincts.

He had to tell Alika what Hamilton had proposed. "Our boss thinks this was Sophie's mother—Hamilton was trying to send me a message before Jenkins threw him into the office." Jake pushed a hand through his hair, considering how much to tell Alika. "Pim Wat has been trying to get Sophie to come to Thailand for a while now. Wants her to work for her spy organization. Sophie has refused. Maybe Pim Wat snatched the baby to get leverage on Sophie."

"That evil bitch! What kind of woman does that to her own child?" Alika's chest expanded. His eyes flashed. Even missing an arm, he was an intimidating sight when he was pissed. "Why wasn't I told any of this?"

"It's classified stuff, man. Need to know. Until now, you didn't need to know."

Alika bunched his fist. "Turns out I did need to know. Anything that has to do with my family is my business."

"Noted." Jake didn't want to engage in the pissing match they'd been dancing around since they first got the news of whose baby Sophie was carrying—the situation was awkward enough. "I'm just glad Hamilton was able to point the cops in another direction."

"We're both going to be in the doghouse for a long time for even imagining Sophie had something to do with our daughter disappearing," Alika said, voicing Jake's worry.

"I better see if the cops will let me talk to her. I'll let Sophie know that we've got evidence that Momi was taken by a third party. That might help." Jake didn't feel too hopeful.

Alika clapped him on the back with his remaining hand. "Better you than me, man."

CHAPTER FIVE

Day Nine

SOPHIE LAY IN BED, curved around her empty belly and aching breasts, the comforter over her head to shut out the light, a return to old habits. She held the yellow flannel sheet that had covered the baby's bassinet mattress folded close in her arms and bundled beneath her chin.

If she shut her eyes, she could inhale the smell of her baby, milky and sweet, still clinging to the bedding. She could pretend that none of the horror of the last hours had happened.

Sophie had cried until she was an empty husk, unable to answer questions from the investigator from KPD who'd implied that she might have had something to do with Momi's disappearance. She'd been unable to defend herself coherently last night. Alika had eventually contacted the doctor they'd had on call for the birth after she'd wrecked the sideboard and Jake had to restrain her.

Jake and Alika had let her down. They were supposed to have her back! Instead, they'd both at least considered that she might have had something to do with Momi's disappearance.

The doctor's eyes had been kind as he checked her over privately in her room upstairs. "Are you sure you want to do this?" he'd asked when she told him to give her a shot to help dry up her milk more quickly. "If the baby is returned soon, you may not be able to nurse her."

"She won't be returned soon." Sophie knew that in her bones.

Her mother had taken her child.

Nothing else made sense. Awful as it was, Sophie was sure of it, and she would need all of her strength and focus in the days to come.

"I need to be able to help find my child. That's the priority. Can you put me on an antidepressant medication, too? I expect I will be having some difficulty." The last thing Sophie needed was a bout of postpartum blues.

A call to Dr. Wilson, Sophie's therapist, had confirmed her diagnosis of chronic depression, and the physician had agreed to write her a script. Esther, the only person Sophie currently trusted, had promptly gone to a nearby pharmacy to fill it.

Those things taken care of, Sophie had taken the tranquilizer the doctor recommended, and gone to bed.

She had allowed herself this one night to wallow.

One night to cry because she hadn't been able to revel in her bond with her child and nurture her daughter with her own milk.

One night to weep that she couldn't enjoy the love of the unconventional family that surrounded her.

One night to be immersed in rage and grief and revenge fantasies about what she'd do to whomever had taken her baby—*even if that person was her mother.*

And now that night was over. There was nothing in her life from here on out but getting Momi back.

Sophie sat up slowly, forcing her aching body to rise. She got up to use the bathroom and change her pads. She paused upon returning, and frowned.

She'd been sleeping so heavily that she hadn't noticed that Jake had joined her in the bed at some point. He hadn't been with her last night, but he was breathing heavily in sleep now, on his side of the bed. His back was to her, the bulky triangle of his shoulder a mountain-like shadow in the dim light seeping through the drapes.

Jake had thought she might have done something to Momi.

Alika had thought so too, though the baby's father hadn't been stupid enough to say so. The cops had all implied it, grilling her over and over again with the same questions, hardly doing a perfunctory check of the grounds outside—and Sophie knew what they'd looked for so hastily: a hole in the dirt where she might have buried her child, some sign she'd tossed the baby off the cliff or smothered her in the laundry basket.

Just the thought made Sophie nauseous.

She turned away from her lover and walked to the window, moving the curtain aside to peek out into the brightness of midmorning. Today she would get ahold of Connor and find a way to get out of this house and look for Momi. Connor would understand, and he would help her without question. He'd never believe she could have done something to Momi.

The bed creaked as Jake got up. She heard his feet pad across the wide teak planks of the floor. She felt the warmth of his body, normally so welcome, against her back in the thin cotton gown she'd been wearing since the birth. His hands cupped her shoulders tentatively. "Hey."

She shrugged him off. "Get away from me."

"I have news." Jake moved back and she felt the loss of heat. "About Momi."

Sophie spun to face him, and the sudden movement made her dizzy. She grasped the windowsill to stabilize, meeting his silver-gray eyes. "I'm listening."

"The cops and Alika and I did a more thorough search early this morning after Hamilton came in and threw his weight around. We found a footprint outside the downstairs office window—too small to be a man's. Also, evidence of a surveillance camp that had been checking out the house. A multi-passenger chopper was parked on the cliff and took off."

"My mother," Sophie said. "I knew it." She felt a strange kind of relief to have it confirmed; at least her mother probably wouldn't harm Momi. The baby would be all right until Sophie could get her back—though Sophie had no idea how steep the price would be.

"Hamilton thinks it was Pim Wat, too." Jake slid a hand up her arm. "I'm so sorry. For what I implied." He squeezed her bicep gently. "I was wrong. The cops were wrong."

"I don't forgive you," Sophie said. "You know my deepest fears and wounds and insecurities, and you judged me by them. Please don't touch me." Her voice sounded wooden and stilted. She felt frozen, a pillar of ice.

Jake dropped his hand and stepped back. "We're not done talking about this."

"I'm done talking about it." She narrowed her eyes. "Where's Hamilton? I need to speak with him."

"Funny. Hamilton was demanding to see you as well, but I told everyone you needed your rest." Jake ran a hand through his hair. "I know I messed up. We have to get past this."

Sophie turned away and walked toward her closet, ignoring his comment. Jake went on. "Hamilton really shook things up and got the investigation headed in the right direction. We all owe him for that."

"At least he believed in me." A spike of rage tightened Sophie's belly. Connor was a white man, loaded with money and authority, arriving in a car with a driver, calm and collected—not a hysterical new mother with a history of depression. The sexism was blatant and repulsive. That she'd needed Connor to intervene made Sophie want to hit someone—Jake, specifically. "Give me some privacy, please. I'm changing."

"Seriously? I've seen it all, Sophie. Been with you as you delivered a baby, for God's sake. Consider all we've been through before you just kick me out." Jake's voice vibrated with hurt and outrage.

Sophie kept her back to him, standing stiffly. "I'm changing, Jake. Please leave."

He left.

Sophie found a tight running bra and wedged herself into it, inserting pads to sop up leaks. She pulled on yoga pants and a black Security Solutions polo that hadn't fit around her girth in five months. As she sat on the bed and bent over to tie on running shoes, her soft, squishy belly got in the way. She pushed at it and felt a gush of fluid from down below. *"Bitch goddess in charge of hell."*

She had to change her pads—again. Giving birth wasn't, apparently, something you just got up and walked away from with no side effects.

Sophie took care of the necessary things, and then packed the bag she'd arrived with a couple of weeks ago. She put her laptop and tablet in the backpack that had always served in lieu of a purse, and, carrying the loaded duffel, she stood in the doorway of the room, looking back at the place where she'd given birth and spent one beautiful night with her baby girl.

What an incredible, unforgettable, intense experience. And it's true, Jake had been with her every challenging minute of it. He'd never flinched or wavered. He'd been her rock.

Sophie's eyes teared up as she spotted the yellow flannel sheet from the bassinet tangled in the bedclothes. She hurried back and picked up the cloth, burying her face in the soft flannel for a moment. The baby's smell caused her sensitive, sore breasts to tingle as milk let down. *"Devilish female parts,"* she swore. Fortunately, she had on the breast shields and the tight bra; the problem would go away within a week, the doctor had said.

Sophie slipped the precious flannel into her backpack and zipped it up. She shut the door and walked quietly to the landing, hearing the murmur of unfamiliar voices down in the great room below.

The cops were still here, and she hadn't given her statement yesterday.

Sophie hid the backpack and her duffel behind a large ceramic potted palm on the upper landing. She descended the stairs, proud of how steady she was on her feet. Ignoring the sound of talking coming from the great room, she went into the kitchen.

She needed strong tea, and lots of it, to deal with what lay ahead.

Esther was washing dishes at the sink and turned to Sophie with a smile. "My dear. You're ready for action, I see."

"Yes. I'm getting Momi back." Sophie approached the older woman, and embraced her from the side as Esther's hands were still deep in suds. "Thank you for believing in me. You were the only one who didn't think I did something to Momi."

Esther had bequeathed large, expressive brown eyes to her grandson Alika, and now those familiar eyes fixed on Sophie's face. "You mustn't blame the boys too much. They were in terrible shock, too."

Sophie pulled back. "But I do blame them, Esther. They judged me as unstable."

"Pause for a moment, *ku'uipo*. If Jake, or Alika for that matter, had fallen asleep with the baby and then woken to find her gone, wouldn't there have been suspicion upon them? Especially Jake. Momi is not his," Esther said gently. She turned back to the dishes. "There is tea beside the stove."

The woman always seemed to know what Sophie was thinking.

CHAPTER SIX

Day Nine

"YOU'RE LOOKING BETTER, today, Ms. Smithson." Detective Jack Jenkins had been home and had a shower and a change of clothes to judge by the comb tracks in his short gelled blond hair. The young man's eyes were candid as he assessed Sophie.

Hearing her maiden name still gave Sophie a tiny twinge of surprise. She'd gone through the necessary steps to change her name legally prior to Momi's birth—it had been past time to close the chapter of her life that had involved her early and disastrous marriage to Assan Ang. "Thank you. I am ready to make a statement."

"Good. Your friend Lei called. She was my partner here on Kaua'i at one time, and she spoke of you highly." He gestured toward Alika's office, which he seemed to have taken over. Clearly, Lei's call had made a difference in his attitude—he'd been respectful but suspicious before. Now he seemed almost solicitous.

"Lei is a good friend." Sophie avoided any eye contact with Jake, Alika, or the officers in the room, and preceded the man inside.

Jenkins set a recorder on the edge of Alika's drafting table, and

Sophie took a seat across from him. He stated the date and time, people present and their location, then addressed Sophie. "State your name for the record."

"Sophie Malee Smithson."

"You have the right to remain silent. Anything you say can and will be used against you in a court of law, and you have the right to an attorney," Jenkins said conversationally.

Sophie frowned. "You're still considering me a suspect?"

"Just covering my bases." Jenkins had the grace to look down and fiddle with his yellow legal pad.

Sophie shook her head. "I would never do anything to hurt my daughter. Ever." The perspective that Esther had given her in the kitchen had shifted the stone of anger sitting on her chest a little, though, and she breathed easier in spite of Jenkins' words. *The evidence would back her up.* "I would like to tell you about my mother, Pim Wat."

"Go on." Jenkins didn't seem surprised at this seeming tangent. *Good.* Perhaps Jake or Connor had already told him something about her mysterious and deadly parent.

"My mother and I were estranged for nine years. Out of the blue, as they say, Pim Wat contacted me close to a year ago, trying to recruit me to join an espionage agency called the Yām Khûmkạn. I have been negotiating with her ever since. Pim Wat has been trying to get me to go to the organization's headquarters in Thailand from the beginning, and I have refused. Now I believe she's taken my child to use as leverage to get me to go."

"Why don't you want to go to this place?"

"I've seen it." Sophie rubbed the scar on her cheek, the site of a gunshot wound rebuilt with skin grafts and a prosthetic cheekbone. "The organization's compound is located in an undeveloped jungle area in Thailand. It's extremely remote, fortified, and filled with hostiles. I do not trust my mother not to have a . . . plan for me." Pim Wat's first arrangement for Sophie, marriage to Assan Ang, had almost killed her.

"Really extreme for a grandma to kidnap her own grandchild." Jenkins tipped his head to the side skeptically. "So far, all we know is that someone took your baby, and the snatch involved a helicopter and multiple perps."

"Pim Wat and I don't have a . . . normal relationship." Sophie rubbed the scar, grounded by the feel of the ridged line of it against the pads of her fingertips. "She married my ambassador father for political reasons. They divorced when I was old enough to attend boarding school. Throughout my childhood, Mother feigned a crippling depression." Sophie could have sworn her mother really did suffer from depression, but the Pim Wat she'd reconnected with seemed symptom-free.

"Really interesting information, Ms. Smithson. And though we've found evidence of an external break-in, there's been absolutely nothing that gives any indication who might actually be involved," Jenkins repeated.

Sophie flicked her fingers. "I'd be surprised if you did find anything tying this directly to Pim Wat—she is cagey and well-versed in covering her tracks. If you've found anything, it's because she didn't care if you did."

"This all seems pretty out there. We'll just have to wait and see."

Sophie crossed her arms over her breasts, but the pressure was too painful so she dropped them to her waist. Unfortunately, that hurt too. "I'm sure Mr. Hamilton told you that Security Solutions would be working on the situation."

"This is a police matter, Ms. Smithson."

"And kidnap rescue is a whole branch of the Security Solutions business," Sophie retorted. "We are specialists, though I hope we won't have to do much more than wait for a call from my mother. Once we have confirmation of a location where my baby is, the crisis is over from a police standpoint—it's a family matter. Now, is there anything else you need from me at this time?"

"Is there anyone else you can think of who might want to take your child?"

Sophie shut her eyes for a moment, pausing to consider. She opened them and met Jenkins's blue gaze. "All of those who have meant me harm are now dead."

The young detective looked spooked. "We'll be in touch, Ms. Smithson. Stay available and in the area."

Sophie had no intention of doing any such thing.

CHAPTER SEVEN

Day Nine, Evening

STANDING in front of the mansion, Sophie faced Alika, her gaze meeting his warm brown eyes. "Are you sure you are okay with this arrangement?"

Alika squeezed her shoulder with his remaining hand. "Do I have a choice? Someone has to hold down the fort and deal with the cops."

"I know. Thank you." Sophie swayed toward him—normally she'd give him a hug, but she was still bitter about his supposition against her. "I will get our daughter back."

"You'd better." Alika turned and walked back up the bluestone steps to stand beside Esther, watching from the porch.

Sophie, Jake, and Connor hurried across the swath of open lawn to where Thom had the Security Solutions chopper waiting, rotors whirling as it warmed up. Sophie raised her hand in farewell, and the two waved back.

Connor got in front with the pilot, while Sophie and Jake stowed their gear bags and sat in the rear jump seats. Jake handed her a helmet, and they both strapped in.

Sophie avoided eye contact with Jake, turning away from him as much as possible to look out the window of the helicopter as it lifted off. The bird wheeled in place, then flew over the Hanalei Valley and out to sea, headed for Honolulu Airport on Oahu where the Security Solutions corporate jet awaited.

As she always did, Sophie scanned the cobalt water for signs of whales, her mind ticking over the day's events.

The police had departed only an hour before. Jenkins handed out his card a second time, and the cruisers were finally gone. Connor had called the three of them into the mansion's office for a quick planning meeting.

"I have already tracked the chopper that flew out from the bluff. It didn't file a flight plan, and that triggered an aviation alert that went out over the FAA airwaves that I was able to track. The chopper landed at Honolulu Airport, and I was able to find it using the surveillance cams." Connor had their full attention, and his fingers flew on his tablet as he surfed the web while talking. "The passengers were gone, and the bird was a rental. I had a Security Solutions agent go and track down the pilot. The man said he had signed an NDA, but a little grease got him talking." Connor looked up and met Sophie's eyes. His gaze was intense, his handsome face set in cold lines—the Ghost in work mode. "The people who rented the chopper were Thai, and consisted of three men and two women. The pilot spotted a baby in a yellow blanket on the way back from Kaua'i."

"Then we have our confirmation that it was my mother," Sophie said.

"Most likely. The physical description that he gave matched her height and looks. The other woman was unknown, and she was the one carrying the baby."

"Probably Armita, my mother's maid. She was my caregiver when I was a young child. Armita must have been the one to snatch Momi." Sophie's belly clenched at the thought of her beloved childhood nanny looking down at Sophie sleeping, then cold-bloodedly taking her child. "Armita climbs and moves like a ninja. That is why the dogs didn't bark—they know her. And my mother."

Sophie told the men about the time Armita had mysteriously visited Sophie on the Big Island, climbing three balconies outside of Sophie's building to do so. "Armita is controlled by Pim Wat, but she had come to warn me that my mother was planning something. I have to wonder if this was what Pim Wat was planning? But Mother hadn't known I was pregnant at that time, so I'm not sure what it could have been."

They'd wrapped up the meeting with a plan to get closer to the Yām Khûmkạn and look for the baby and Pim Wat from Connor's base of operations on his private island in Thailand. Hopefully, Pim Wat would make contact soon and be forthcoming with her demands for returning the baby.

That brought Sophie to now: to the soreness of her full breasts, the emptiness of her arms, the betrayal of her beloved nanny and less beloved mother, and the uncertainty of the mission ahead. She blinked, looking at but not seeing the whitecaps scudding over the windswept ocean.

Jake tried to take her hand, but she pulled it away without looking at him.

CHAPTER EIGHT

Day Ten

Sophie, Jake, Connor, Thom, and Kiefer Rhinehart, commander of Security Solutions' elite kidnap rescue squad, sat around a long polished teak table in the dining room of Connor's house on Phi Ni. Anubis, Connor's dignified Doberman, sat in watchful silence observing them as they organized everything for their meeting.

Sophie had been to Connor's cliffside aerie before, so she was used to the beauty of the custom-made home high on the bluffs. Seeing it fresh through Jake's and Rhinehart's eyes, she didn't blame the men for the awed silence with which they'd first viewed the mansion, an exquisite rendering in native wood and stone, a perfect marriage of cultures.

Nam, Connor's houseman, had set up a projection screen on one wall of the dining room along with a whiteboard. Connor lowered burnished metal, bulletproof blinds to cut the sun streaming through floor-to-ceiling sliding doors that provided a brilliant and distracting view of turquoise sea and tiny, fertile atolls far below the bluffs on which the house was perched.

He projected a satellite photo of the Yām Khûmkạn's elaborate stone temple stronghold onto the white screen. He flicked on a laser pointer and pointed out the main building, a pyramid-like structure of elaborately carved, lichen-covered stone. "I have been trying, since Pim Wat began attempting to recruit Sophie to go to this stronghold, to get eyes and ears inside this place—but it's the most locked down fortress I've come across. Everyone who goes in or out has some loyalty or association with the Yām Khûmkạn, and they are feared. I can't find anyone to take my bribes." Connor glanced at Rhinehart. "Thoughts?"

"We often don't have much on the place where the target is being held, but that's never stopped us before." Rhinehart was a fireplug of a man, heavily muscled as if making up for lack of height with breadth. A low-slung jaw and cauliflower ears completed the visage of a thug, but Rhinehart's small brown eyes glittered with intelligence. "We still haven't heard what the takers want."

Sophie lifted a finger to get the table's attention. "If by 'takers' you mean my mother, we may not hear from her at all. I gave this a lot of thought on the way over. Best case scenario: Pim Wat wants something specific from me, something she's been trying to get since she contacted me. I'll hear from her about that, and we'll move forward with some kind of negotiation."

"You will not go into danger at that fortress," Jake said through his teeth.

Sophie ignored him, holding up her finger. "Or, Pim Wat won't contact me. She has my daughter for herself for whatever reason. I may never hear from my mother."

Everyone stilled at these words. Sophie went on. "Pim Wat has been frustrated with me for years now. She has repeatedly told me I am not the biddable child I was, clay to be molded to her wishes. Perhaps she simply took my baby and means to raise her instead."

"Nasty thought." Rhinehart inclined his buzz-cut head in Sophie's direction. "But not out of the realm of possibility with this woman, though she hardly seems the nurturing type, with the patience to raise a newborn."

"You forget. She has Armita, my former nanny," Sophie said. "Pim Wat can have all of the benefits and none of the hard work of raising a child with my baby in Armita's capable hands." Her nanny's betrayal still hurt more than it should.

Rhinehart nodded. "I had time to read the file Mr. Hamilton has assembled on your mother on the way over, and . . . she's a real piece of work, if you don't mind my saying. This kidnapping isn't the usual grab for cash we deal with."

"It's not. It never was," Connor looked back down at his tablet. "We still have satellite imagery and can map the stronghold from the outside. I've also been able to use some leverage on one of the Yām Khûmkạn's kitchen suppliers to get a bug into the place. Unfortunately, he planted it in a shitty area. They have signal dampeners in place, so I can't even get that data out."

"Let's move forward as if we know she's in there," Jake said. "How are we going to penetrate and get Momi out?"

The discussion was long.

Nam brought in steaming plates of rice, fish, and vegetables, and they ate while working. Rhinehart, taking the lead, drew approach ideas on clear Plexiglas set over a blown-up satellite image of the compound and the surrounding jungle.

Sophie, who hadn't slept during the entire eighteen-hour flight, felt exhaustion pulling at her limbs. Her breasts throbbed—she had to do something about the milk hardening them. "I need to get some rest. I will be back in a couple of hours."

"Let me walk you to our room." Jake got up and followed Sophie into the beautiful courtyard with its fountain statue of Quan Yin surrounded by tropical plants. Sophie led him to the guest quarters she'd occupied before, a large, airy room with an attached seating area and a sliding glass door leading out to a balcony overlooking a spectacular view.

Her bag rested on one side of the bed, and Jake's on the other—Nam had brought their belongings in when they arrived. Sophie stared at the bags, wondering what to do next.

Depression lapped at Sophie's consciousness, black oil coating her thoughts. *She needed to take that little white pill* . . .

"I would ask Hamilton to put you in another room, but there aren't any with the extra people here." Sophie took her duffel off the bed and set it on a chair. She unzipped it and took out a breast pump. "I'd appreciate some privacy."

"Come on, Sophie." Jake sat on the edge of the bed, immovable as a boulder. "Remember, I've seen it all. Touched it all. Tasted it all, as a matter of fact." She shot him a narrowed glare, but he just grinned. "Don't hold onto being mad. We need each other. Momi needs her parents united, not fighting."

Her parents. He said it so naturally. He really did consider Momi his, as much as Alika's. Sophie sat down slowly on the bed. "You thought I might have killed my baby."

"I didn't. I thought . . ." Jake leaned forward, pushing big hands into his hair, rubbing up and down through the short dark strands. "I thought maybe you sleepwalked. Had a fugue state. I don't know! I was looking for an explanation. Never did I think you'd have consciously harmed our baby."

"Not good enough." Sophie unbuttoned her blouse and contemplated the wall-like exercise bra flattening her breasts. She pried the bra down to expose one of them, as jutting and hard as if it were in rigor. She applied the plastic suction cup to her nipple and turned the pump on. The apparatus rumbled in her hand, and she winced as suction dragged at her swollen, painful flesh.

They both watched in fascination as reflex finally kicked in and milk jetted, as if under pressure, into a small holding tank affixed to the pump. Jake's eyes were wide at the sight. "You're gonna need to dump that pretty quick."

"Such a waste." Sophie felt tears prickle. "I hate to just throw this milk away when my body made it for *her*." Saying Momi's name was too difficult.

"You can be a mother to her in other ways," Jake said.

Sophie nodded but couldn't speak past the lump in her throat.

When the catcher was full, Jake took it from her hand and dumped it in the bathroom sink without a word. Sophie did the other side, and he dumped that too.

Relief from the milk's pressure felt like another kind of pain. *She wasn't going to cry.* Not anymore. She was done with tears.

"Get some rest. You need it." Jake gave her a gentle push so that she tipped over onto her side, her eyes already closing as her head hit the pillow.

Sophie let him lift the coverlet and cover her. Felt his lips touch her forehead in a gentle kiss. The lights dimmed, the door shut, and he was gone.

So was she.

CHAPTER NINE

Day Ten

ARMITA LOOKED DOWN at the baby's tiny face, relaxed in sleep, the pink bud of her mouth slightly open. Sophie's infant daughter had a full head of glossy black curls, tawny skin, and features that hinted at future beauty. Armita traced the baby's downy cheek, and Momi's plump lips turned to follow the touch, making Armita smile.

Momi would lack for nothing, not even human milk. Armita had arranged for a woman from a nearby village to come in and provide that, and now the wet nurse had gone back to the kitchens.

Her heart still pounded when she thought of the day Pim Wat had taken Momi, and her arms tightened around the baby as memory transported her back to the scene.

She and the pilot had been waiting two days on the bluff in the scrim of Java plum trees for Pim Wat and her soldiers to return with Sophie Malee. Armita had checked the adult-sized emergency transport pod in the helicopter over and over: the oxygen tank, the coverings, and restraints. *Everything had to be perfect.* Sophie Malee would be unconscious, and they had to monitor her carefully on the flight because of the pregnancy.

Suddenly Pim Wat had appeared, bursting out of the trees at a run. She was carrying a yellow-wrapped bundle in her arms, and the soldiers behind her were empty-handed but for their weapons. *Where was Sophie Malee?*

Pim Wat reached the helicopter, and the soldier closest opened the side door for her and gave her a hand up the step. Pim Wat thrust the bundle at Armita, speaking in Thai. "Hold this."

Armita gasped, looking down at a tiny crumpled face framed in the yellow blanket. "Mistress! What is going on? Where is Sophie Malee?"

Pim Wat's face was expressionless as she took her seat and buckled into the four-point harness. "Sophie Malee gave birth early. Easier to take the child than to deal with my daughter. Now that we have the baby, we don't need her."

Armita sat frozen as the men assumed their seats. "But . . . we *do* need Sophie Malee. She is the baby's *mother.*" Armita's heart thudded and her hands sweated as the pilot warmed up the engine. She tucked the baby between her neck and shoulder, clasping it close.

"We will stop on the next island and get formula to feed it. The child will be fine." Pim Wat barked orders at the pilot as she donned her helmet with its built-in comm. "What's wrong with you, Armita? Put on your helmet and harness."

Armita clutched the newborn tightly as the speed of the rotors increased and the sound of the engine rose to a roar. She pressed the baby's head against her chest, covering the infant's delicate ears to protect them from the tremendous sound. She could not bring herself to put the child down, even to take care of necessary safety details.

One of the soldiers, his expression softening slightly, picked up Armita's helmet and put it on her, buckling the strap under her chin, then securing the four-point harness over her arms as she held the baby against her.

G-forces pressed them into their seats as the helicopter rose rapidly and then spun, arrowing out from its hiding place, soon reaching top speed over the nearby ocean.

Armita closed her eyes. Grief swamped her for the suffering her former ward would feel upon the disappearance of her newborn. She snuggled the baby as if through that contact she could somehow comfort the infant's mother, too. And in the shadow cast by her helmet, Armita surveyed Pim Wat.

Her mistress's striking countenance was turned toward the window. Her indifference was palpable; all she cared about was returning to the Master.

Pim Wat had no compassion, not a breath of love in her body for her own daughter or grandchild, let alone the poor maid who had tried to serve her all these years.

It wasn't right.

Armita had felt the baby wriggle, the vibration of its tiny cry, the touch of its lips rooting against her neck as she held it in the chaos of the helicopter's flight. She closed her eyes and breathed in the child's tender, unforgettable milky smell. "I will protect you, little one. I will find a way to bring you home."

And she would do that, even if it killed her in the end.

All of that had led to this moment, and Armita had no regrets. She had reached the end of what she would tolerate from Pim Wat. Sophie's daughter had her loyalty now.

CHAPTER TEN

Day Eleven

SOPHIE STRETCHED, and the dull ache of her body gradually brought her into awareness—but even so, she felt rested. She'd slept a long time.

She stared up at the woven natural fiber lattice of the ceiling, wondering at the achiness of her body—and recognized her room in Connor's house on Phi Ni, Thailand.

Her daughter was missing.

Sophie surged up so quickly that she fell out of bed, landing on the pandanus matting covering the floor. She groaned as she got up more slowly, rising to hands and knees, then gradually standing.

Someone had closed the blackout curtains over the sliding glass doors, likely Jake.

She drew the curtain aside and recoiled from the brightness of sea, sky, and sand on the other side of the balcony far below. She let the curtain fall, frowning—Jake's bag was gone, and his pillow beside hers, undented. *He must have found other accommodation after all.*

Pain in her chest—Sophie hadn't really meant for him to leave. She would have to find him and tell him that.

But first, her breasts were causing her agony.

Sophie went to the bathroom and did her business, expressing just enough milk to relieve the pain, pleased that various leakages were much decreased. She palpated her belly as she looked in the mirror—even that was subsiding a bit, and hurt much less today.

She was a long way from fighting fit, but she was also a lot closer than she'd been the day before.

The silence of the house penetrated Sophie's awareness.

The men must be outside, packing or putting together their gear and weapons. *How long had she been sleeping?* She checked the clock beside the bed. *"Son of a snake charmer!"* She'd been out for close to twenty hours!

Sophie dressed quickly in a fresh exercise bra and nursing pads, yoga pants, a tank top, and wet/dry hiking shoes. She zipped up her duffel, slung it onto her shoulder, and exited the room.

Anubis, Connor's beautiful Doberman, sat outside her door. "Hey, boy." She greeted the dignified dog with a head rub. "Where's your master?"

"Woof," Anubis replied, and fell into step beside her, moving with springy grace.

Connor's house was a square laid out around a central courtyard. She walked down the hall to the front entrance. Glossy woods, sculptures, and vista views alike passed by her unnoticed. "Hamilton? Jake?" Her voice echoed around the stone-flagged entry.

"Ms. Smithson." Nam had always refused to call her by her first name, and now the dignified houseman tripped over her new last name. "They are gone."

"What?" Sophie pulled herself up to her full five foot nine as rage and alarm flushed her system. Her bag dropped off her shoulder to hit the ground. "What did you say?"

"You slept for twenty hours, miss. The men went to the mainland to get your baby. Mr. Hamilton, he left you a message."

"No. They wouldn't." Sophie had always thought the phrase "seeing red" was some American slang, but now her vision actually was clouded by the color. All she wanted to do was smash something.

In a plain black tunic, narrow leggings, and felt-bottomed shoes, his face blank, Nam reminded her of one of the inscrutable stone lions that guarded the front door. "I'm sorry, miss."

"Demon spawn of a pox-ridden whore!" Sophie balled her fists. *"Swine-born betrayers!"*

"The message is in Mr. Hamilton's office, miss. He did not want the other men to see it." Nam's hands remained folded together over his midriff, his gaze calm.

Sophie ran forward and wrenched open one of the French doors that led into the central courtyard. She flew across the pretty space with its tinkling fountain to the sliding glass door that led into Connor's office.

She spotted the note immediately, resting on the keyboard of the computer rig Connor had set up for her on her last visit. Sophie picked up the note, but her hand was shaking so badly that she could scarcely read his elegant handwriting. She remembered the last time she'd seen his writing; he had left her another note, equally devastating, in a deposit box—a note to be read upon his death.

Which had turned out to be fake, like so much about him. Smoke and mirrors, as her friend Marcella would say. Yet Sophie'd never doubted the feeling behind whatever words he might have chosen to explain his duplicity, and she didn't doubt them this time, either.

"Dear Sophie,

We thought of waking you. Jake and I talked it over. But when we looked in at you, sleeping deeply, so clearly at the end of your physical resources, we couldn't do it. Even though we both know how angry you are going to be to be excluded from this mission, think about this: what if we fail?

The Yām Khûmkạn fortress is no easy target.

Who will Momi have if we are taken?

I've left information with Nam in case of such a contingency—all you will need to take over Security Solutions and more. I trust you with that, with everything that I have, and with that other secret, too.

You need to recover from the birth. You need time for your body to adjust to all of the changes. And Momi needs a mother to come home to, a mother who is healthy and strong. Because whatever is between you and Pim Wat won't be over when we take her grand-child from her.

Rage all you want—but rest when you are done. Eat well. Use my gym until you are fit again. And be waiting for your daughter when we bring her home to you." ~ Connor

Sophie cursed, long and inventively.

She didn't tear the note up, though. She had done that to the other one, and regretted it. She stuffed the paper into her pocket and began rifling the office, looking for a set of keys, some way to get off the island.

The mission they'd discussed the day before had a two-week timeline. They would be radio silent, unless Connor was sure he could use a satellite internet signal undetected.

Two weeks was an eternity for her to be stuck here, alone, without even an update!

Sophie felt rather than saw Nam standing in the doorway. She spun to face him, and he inclined his upper body in a bow, his hands folded. "Mr. Hamilton has left an ATV for your use."

Sophie put her hands on her hips. "How does that do me any good in following them to the mainland?"

"Perhaps it will satisfy you to explore the island. To evaluate all of its weaknesses and strengths." Nam held out a hand. Resting on it was a set of keys.

Sophie took the keys, pausing to look around the immaculate office, a mirror double to the one she had worked in with Connor before on Oahu. Three computer monitors were set up in a bay. The second set, ones she'd used before, invited her to explore them. Across the room, Connor's Bowflex machine and a steeply inclined treadmill, along with a pull-up bar, indicated what he did to refresh his mind between activities.

Sophie was in no shape for that kind of workout yet—in fact, all of the upset and running around had necessitated another change of pads. *So frustrating.*

She stomped past Nam and went back to her apartment. She dropped her duffel and backpack beside the bed and noticed, for the first time, a small black box weighing down a sealed envelope on Jake's nightstand. *"Stench of an unwashed goat!"*

She was not in the mood to read any further notes, apologies, or declarations of love.

She just wanted her baby back.

Sophie changed her soaked pads, and then hurried through the house and across the gleaming teak floors to head back outside.

The barnlike metal garage where Connor kept his vehicles and sports equipment was locked with a huge padlock, but the ATV was parked beside the shed, pointed down the road that led up the hill to the estate. Sophie marched over to the all-terrain vehicle, swung her leg over, inserted the key, put it in gear, and roared down the long, curving driveway.

CHAPTER ELEVEN

Day Eleven

SOPHIE WENT DOWN every graveled road on the fourteen-mile island, looking for a way off of it.

She found the little farm compound where Nam and his family, seemingly the only other occupants of Phi Ni, lived. Nam's wife, a kind-faced older woman, came to the door, wringing her hands in distress as Sophie roared up to the dwelling.

Sophie raised her hand in a wave, smiling to reassure the woman, and hurried on.

She eventually arrived at the familiar airstrip with its large metal hangar, mechanical maintenance area, and fueling station, and strip of asphalt ending at a beach.

The plane and chopper were both gone. *"Damn those men to an eternity of hungry mosquitoes!"*

Sophie turned the ATV down a bumpy, badly maintained side road leading away from the airstrip, following the sandy dirt track through acres of overgrown palms planted in rows—some sort of coconut plantation from the past. Beyond that, a jungle of trees entangled with vines gave way to a small, deep bay where the road dead-ended. A dock built of heavy wooden pilings topped by a large boathouse projected out into crystalline water.

Sophie's heart speeded up. *At last, a way off the island!*

Sophie drove the ATV out onto the dock and dismounted to investigate. The heavy metal boathouse was locked, the hasp of the door corroded with rust, but the lock on it huge and shiny-new.

"There's more than one way to skin a cat." Terrible saying, but it had captured her imagination. Already overheated in the tropical heat, with not a soul to see her for miles, Sophie stripped down to her underwear and dove into the water off the end of the pier.

The water, clear as glass, felt like a bracing slap to Sophie's face, dispelling the fog of obsessive anger that had driven her. Her aches and pain were forgotten as she swam, weightless and powerful, underwater. She came up and blew out a breath. Her hair, grown long and wild during pregnancy, dripped water into her eyes. Sophie made a mental note to cut it when she returned to the house.

The sting of the salt water on her ravaged tissues was a strange kind of balm, and the buoyancy of floating felt amazing. Sophie reached the end of the boathouse and circled around to the opening that faced outward toward the ocean.

The exterior door was down there, too, but the tide must have been low because there was a foot or two of clearance between where the door ended and the restless surface of the water began. Sophie ducked beneath the segmented gate and swam inside the big shelter.

The boathouse's shadow glowed around her, lit by sunlight bouncing off the sand fifteen feet or so below. Sophie navigated around a sleek speedboat tied to the interior dock, and scanned for a ladder. Sure enough, one led down into the water, and she grasped the metal rungs.

Her body was already trembling with the exertion of the ATV journey from the house on the top of the hill to this point. Her arms trembled as she hoisted her body up out of the water and climbed the ladder. She had done yoga daily until the birth, but had neglected heavier workouts in lieu of relaxation and stretching as her pregnancy progressed.

She had imagined reclaiming her fitness level with the baby beside her, sleeping. A stab of grief and longing filled her, remembering the brightly patterned sling she had planned to use to keep the baby close while she did weights or walking.

"We will get her back," Sophie said aloud. Her voice bounced and echoed in the vast space, punctuated by the slapping of the water against the boat and the pier. "Or die trying."

Not an empty statement. She had no intention of giving up on finding her daughter—ever.

Sophie padded along the wooden pier to the speedboat and jumped aboard a twenty-seven-foot Chris-Craft Corsair. Low-slung, heavy and luxurious, with a powerful inboard engine, a forward berth, and shiny wood and brass fittings, everything about the launch was beautiful. Sophie ran her hands over the glossy burled steering wheel. *Just like Connor to have a boat that would look right at home on the Riviera parked in his boathouse in the middle of nowhere.*

This was how she was going to leave Phi Ni and get to the mainland to find her daughter.

Sophie shook with cold and exertion even in the tropical heat as she explored the boat. She made her way below deck and found a white, waffle-weave robe to don in the berth. She searched everywhere but couldn't find a key, on the boat or around the dock, and the Chris-Craft's sealed navigation area was theft-resistant.

Connor and Jake shouldn't have left her marooned here on Phi Ni. They could have given her surveillance, light duty, something appropriate to do on the mission.

But as Sophie walked back down the interior dock, looking for an exit that didn't involve swimming back out of the boathouse, she was ready to reconsider the situation.

She was stuck on Phi Ni for the moment. Even if she could find keys to the Chris-Craft and get it out of the boathouse, her physical state was unacceptable. Just riding an ATV and swimming a few hundred yards should not have exhausted her this much. She wasn't ready for a jungle combat situation, painful as it was to admit it.

She'd just had a baby. Growing a child and giving birth to it was a huge physical feat that took a toll, whether she was willing to admit it or not.

Sophie found a small side exit door with an interior lock, and opened it. She blinked in the overly bright sunlight, bedazzled for a moment—then her eyes focused on a man standing beside a pickup truck, parked at the end of the dock. Her heart pounded until she recognized Nam, standing backlit, waiting with his typical quiet dignity.

Sophie locked the boathouse door. She picked up her clothing and headed for the houseman, glad she'd covered herself with the boat's handy robe.

"Would you like a ride back to the house?" Nam asked.

"I would." Sophie pointed to the ATV. "What about that?"

Nam walked to the rear of the truck, lowered the tailgate, and pulled out a couple of steel runners. A few moments later, the ATV was stowed in back and they were driving up the mountain.

"A late lunch is waiting for you. Very nutritious, to build up your strength," Nam said. "The fresh vegetables that you like." He had remembered her tastes, from her other visit.

Sophie touched his arm. "Thank you. I'm sorry I was so rude."

He inclined his head. "You miss your baby. I understand."

"I have to get in shape as quickly as possible."

"Of course you do. Mr. Hamilton told me that would be your priority."

"I will need . . ."

"We have everything that you will need," Nam said.

Sophie settled back against the seat and closed her eyes to rest. Workouts would begin that afternoon.

CHAPTER TWELVE

Day Seventeen

JAKE LEANED in close to view the waterproof tablet monitor, his shoulder brushing Hamilton's. Rhinehart was on the move, a camera fixed to his goggles showing them jungle lit green by night vision as the operative worked his way toward the edge of the Yām Khûmkạn's grounds. Using thermal imaging, they'd been able to identify the sentry points around the compound and Rhinehart had already successfully avoided several. His mission, this time, was simple: plant a camera as close to the main temple as possible.

They needed confirmation that the baby was inside, and where exactly she was located.

Jake tightened a fist. *This had to work.* Because so far, nothing else about the mission had gone well.

They'd taken the chopper as far inland as they dared, before landing at a strategic location to be joined by a Security Solutions team of operatives. Five well-trained men with military and law enforcement backgrounds and an arsenal of weapons had rendezvoused with them at the checkpoint, and they'd secured choppers for their return.

Thom Tang had procured their guide, a native man of few words, and those he did speak were in Thai. Hampered by mud, mosquitoes, snakes, and vegetation, they'd worked their way, traveling parallel to a narrow supply road, to within a couple of miles of the compound.

Hamilton had deployed his satellite monitoring, and they'd kept an eye on the stronghold for any unusual activity. So far, there had been nothing to see from above but the daily drilling of the ninjas, first in neat rows, and then in sparring pairs.

"They're not ninjas," Hamilton had said when Jake first called the black-clad martial arts practitioners that. "Just recruits getting brainwashed."

"Don't know what else you'd call them," Rhinehart chimed in. "Those recruits are pretty impressive. Fortunately, we've got firepower like Ol' Betsy here." He'd patted his assault rifle fondly.

"We need to do everything we can to avoid a confrontation," Jake growled. "Our baby is in there, a hostage."

And that was the crux of the matter. They were up against a large group—estimates gleaned from the satellite imagery ranged from one to three hundred. These were trained martial artists with armed guards at every compass point of an ancient stone temple complex— and they had no real idea of where Momi might be stashed inside that heavily guarded maze.

Once they had a visual on the baby, though, they could work on an extraction plan.

Jake swatted a mosquito. When would his body, riddled with welted bites, begin to get used to the little bloodsuckers? Just one of a million discomforts in the current situation. None of it mattered. The mission objective, their baby, was what mattered.

Sophie was probably so pissed at him and Hamilton. Jake pictured Sophie prowling the island looking for escape, enraged and terrified for her child, wanting to kick his ass first and Hamilton's second. Hopefully that stage hadn't lasted too long and she'd moved on to healing and recovering her strength. She'd forgive him when he returned with Momi in his arms . . .

"Steady now," Hamilton whispered, drawing Jake's attention back to the grainy green feed lighting up the tablet. "Steady."

Rhinehart crept around a stone parapet and entered the outer courtyard of the stronghold. He planted a surveillance node on the wall, positioned to take in one of the slit-like doorways. He then sidled inside.

The unlit passageway was so narrow that Rhinehart's sturdy shoulders brushed either side of it. All they heard was the man's rasping breaths, his whispered commentary. "This place is a maze. Don't know how much deeper I can get in here without . . ."

A figure loomed out of the dark and they heard a query in Thai. "Where are you going?"

"To shit," Rhinehart growled back in that same language. A loose cowl over his head concealed his face. "Want to watch?"

The guard grunted and waved him on.

Rhinehart reached an open room lined with beds. Rows of sleeping ninjas on cots filled the space, the sheer number of them making the hair rise on Jake's neck. The operative walked quickly and quietly through the room, headed for an opening on the other side, moving like a man who knew where he was going and why.

Much of getting through other people undetected was moving with confidence, as if you belonged there.

Rhinehart padded down a hallway lit by a flickering torch, eventually reaching a large hall. Tables and benches down the middle of the room showed the room's purpose. "Planting final camera. Target will likely come through at some point," Rhinehart whispered.

"Affirmative," Jake said. "Now get out of there."

Rhinehart jumped up to attach the tiny camera to the lip of the door, and then made his way back through the sleeping quarters. Several close encounters later, the Security Solutions man was on the move, back through the jungle.

Jake frowned. "Seems too easy." He glanced at Hamilton.

The CEO's brows were drawn together and his glasses had slid down his nose. Hamilton took them off with an impatient gesture. "Seems too easy to me, too."

"We'll just have to wait and see, boss."

Hamilton gave a brief nod. "Call me Connor. It's what I go by with my friends."

Friends. In the week that they'd been sharing a tent, meals, and uncomfortable jungle trekking, Jake had found himself respecting Hamilton. The man was cool under pressure, a strategic thinker, and uncomplaining in the physically challenging circumstances of the jungle setting.

"We need to monitor these cameras twenty-four hours a day, Connor. I'll take the first shift. You should get some rest."

Connor gave a brief nod and went to his pallet, sliding into his light sleeping bag.

Jake arranged the different views into a grid and watched the grainy feed. *This was going to get old fast.*

As Rhinehart reached the camp, Jake emerged from the tent he shared with Connor to meet him.

"Got it done." Rhinehart tore off the NV goggles and concealing hood, clearly eager to be rid of the hot and uncomfortable gear.

"Good job, man." Jake clapped him on the back, suppressing his concerns about the ease of the op.

So far, they hadn't seen or detected high tech surveillance equipment in or around the stronghold; a likely reason being the damp conditions that would quickly ruin most electronics. Yes, it felt too easy—but likely the Yām Khûmkạn were getting complacent in their isolation. Would they really have detected Rhinehart and allowed him to roam their base as he had? And then allow their fortress to be bugged?

The answer was simple: they wouldn't. *Don't look a gift horse in the mouth, Jake.*

"Get some rest, Rhinehart. We'll meet tomorrow to review a plan for when we have confirmation that the target is on the grounds," Jake said.

The other man nodded and headed for his tent. Jake watched him go thoughtfully, and switched off the small LED perimeter light providing minimal illumination to the campsite. Sentries at their perimeter provided an extra layer of protection.

The target. Jake couldn't afford to feel all the love and worry that churned within him: the utter lack of anything soft or nurturing in the motives of the black-hearted woman who'd stolen her own grandchild, worry about the environmental threats to a tiny newborn in that dank-looking stone fortress, the many unknown germs. Calling Momi "the target" helped him shut all that out and just think of the objective.

There had to be more to the interior of the stronghold than what they'd seen so far. He couldn't imagine a pampered woman like Pim Wat tolerating the primitive conditions of the barracks, practice courtyards, and spartan dining area they'd been able to get a look at.

There must be somewhere softer and more civilized, and someone other than Pim Wat to hold his daughter close and keep the baby warm, fed, and nurtured, physically and emotionally. Hopefully, that person was the mysterious nanny, Armita, that Sophie had referred to. Sophie clearly felt betrayed by the woman's involvement in the baby's disappearance, but trusted her to take care of Momi better than her mother would.

Jake watched the grainy surveillance video of the interior of the fortress until his eyes were burning. His muscles cramped as he continued to do isometric exercises to keep his body busy and awake.

A hand grasped his shoulder, startling him. "Time for shut-eye, Jake."

"Thanks." Jake handed over the tablet. "Something is bound to show up soon."

"We won't stop looking until it does." Connor's dark hair was mussed and his glasses were back in place. Even wearing jungle camo, the guy managed to look like he was modeling for a clothing catalog.

Warmed by his friend's words, Jake went to his bed and fell into a depthless sleep.

CHAPTER THIRTEEN

Day Twenty-Two

CONNOR ROLLED his shoulders back and tightened his abs, raising his feet off the ground as he pushed up with his arms, lifting his feet out in front of him, parallel to the ground. Ahead of him, he watched the surveillance feed of the interior of the Yām Khûmkạn stronghold on the tablet.

Jake had shown him some of the isometric workout exercises he was so fond of, and doing some of them while watching the live stream helped control his frustration—but barely. The mind-numbing surveillance could be so much better done by hooking it into Security Solutions' AI nanny cam software, but there was no way to train the system without developing a typical baseline. He'd begun gathering that information in case they were here long enough to enable that system—a terrible thought. They were running out of food and supplies.

This trip had a two-week window, and they were nearing the end of it.

Connor had sent short text messages to Sophie and Bix, apprising them of progress. But five days after the planting of the cameras, he and Jake still didn't have any confirmation on Momi's location. No ransom or other demand had come through, either, according to Sophie—so they had no alternative idea of where to look for the baby.

Connor mulled over the activity of the last few days.

The men had continued to optimize their situation, moving closer to the stronghold until they'd found a mounded hillock above swampy ground that was screened with vegetation to hide their camping area. Jake had supervised the setup of electronic perimeter alerts and a rotating two-man watch detail. And then they'd settled in to wait and watch for a sign of Momi's presence, some confirmation of where they could retrieve her.

The hours spent battling boredom and mosquitoes dragged.

Not having his computer eyes and ears, just this one grainy window into the building, was driving Connor nuts—along with a rising conviction.

He'd made a grave error coming on this mission. His time would have been much better spent on Phi Ni, monitoring the situation from a safe distance with high-speed internet. The Ghost could have kept working in the background, looking for other ways in, other places the baby might be.

He'd been driven by emotion when he came on the op; he hadn't been thinking clearly about the best use of resources. But this situation couldn't go on for much longer . . .

As if that thought had conjured it—BAM! Something blew Connor backward into the fabric of the tent.

Darkness.

CONNOR CAME BACK to consciousness in stages.

Shouting.

The rattle of nearby gunfire.

Connor curled onto his side, covering his ears with his hands, shutting his eyes instinctively.

The weapons fire stopped.

Thank God. That shit was *loud,* and his head was already pounding like a *taiko* drum.

Another detonation, right near him this time.

Light flashed red behind his eyelids. More blackness.

He was being dragged. By the back of his shirt. His cheek scraped and banged on the dirt. Whoever was dragging him was yelling in Thai. He struggled to assign meaning to the rapid, liquid sounds of the language: *"Bring the rest of them. Put them in a line."*

They'd been captured.

Adrenaline surged through Connor in a potent wave. He pulled in his center of gravity, yanking in his arms and legs. He thrust up to stand, wrenching his shirt out of his attacker's hand. He spun around to run—*if he got away, he could get help.*

Powerful LED lamps switched on suddenly, blinding him, throwing the jungle into sharp relief and giving a surreal look to the scene.

Ninjas three deep faced him on every side, their black outfits menacing, their weapons even more so.

Connor went down under pummeling fists and feet, and was soon forced into a ragged line with the remaining survivors.

He, Jake, Thom Tang, two remaining Security Solutions operatives named Snowman and Davies, and Rhinehart were the only ones left alive from the blitz attack that had overwhelmed their camp.

The ninjas secured their hands and feet with zip ties and pushed and prodded them until all of the men sat up on their knees.

Jake, beside Connor and last in the row, spat blood on the ground. He had a huge shiner swelling one eye, but his grin was untamed. "Not bad for a civilian. Took four of them to bring you back into the lineup."

"Too little, too late," Connor said darkly. He had a bad feeling about the way they were lined up.

"They'll negotiate our release," Jake said. "Let Rhinehart do the talking. He's good at what he does."

Rhinehart, first in the lineup, looked battered but confident—his powerful shoulders looked relaxed, his head held high, gleaming in the electronic lamps' light.

Connor felt a little of the tension torquing his muscles leach out. *The members of his team were pros and were used to dealing with situations like this.*

The roar of an ATV brought their heads around to face an arriving vehicle. A petite female figure all in black got off the back of the vehicle piloted by a hulking ninja slung about with automatic weapons.

The woman strode into the light, and the lithe way she moved reminded Connor of Sophie. Exquisitely beautiful in her black ninja outfit, her tawny skin glowing in the arc lights, Pim Wat drew every eye. She didn't appear to be armed.

Silence fell. The ninjas went still. Pim Wat raked the row of them with her dark gaze, and Connor's mouth dried.

"Who speaks for you?" Pim Wat said.

"I do," Rhinehart replied. Even kneeling, he looked strong and capable. "We can work something out."

"Where is my daughter?" Pim Wat reached over her shoulder. She drew a samurai sword out of a back scabbard with a slithering sound. *She was armed after all.*

"We can discuss that. We will need to negotiate for that information, though . . ."

Pim Wat took a step past Rhinehart to stand in front of Davies. The man didn't even have a chance to beg for his life before Pim Wat brought the sword down in a slashing arc, eviscerating him. As Davies opened his mouth to scream, looking down at his entrails spilling in disbelief, she decapitated him with a single blow.

Davies' head hit the ground with a wet thump. Arterial blood sprayed the men on either side of him.

A cacophony of yelling and panic erupted as Snowman, on the

other side of Davies, instinctively tried to escape and was manhandled back into line.

Pim Wat stood quietly, her blade dripping. Her gaze moved down the row of them to fall on Jake—and then, horrifyingly, landed on Connor. Recognition flared her eyes wide. A delighted smile lit her blood-spattered face. "Sophie's lovers! Oh, how delightful!"

Pim Wat turned back to Rhinehart and her smile was pure poison this time. "I don't need any of the rest of you now. I have something my daughter will want as much as her child, and these two men will give me all the information I need."

Pim Wat swung the sword.

Rhinehart's head joined Davies', and Snowman's.

She reached Thom Tang. She hadn't even bothered to wipe her sword between executions. *"NO!"* Connor cried out involuntarily.

The diminutive Thai pilot had closed his eyes, his face pale as he awaited his fate stoically. Thom had been more than a pilot and driver to Connor—he'd been a *friend,* and Connor had precious few of them.

Pim Wat paused. Her beautiful dark eyes flashed as they met his. "Where is my daughter, Mr. Hamilton?"

Jake bumped Connor with his shoulder to get Connor's attention, and glared at him. *He couldn't tell Sophie's location!*

"Sophie is safe," Connor said.

Pim Wat's face twisted into something ugly. "I need to know where my daughter is. Tell me and I will spare this man's life."

Connor groped for something to sway her. "Please. Thom is a good man with a family. Not a soldier or a killer. He never signed up for this life."

"Give me what I want and he can be as good or bad as he pleases."

Thom turned his head and met Connor's gaze. The pilot's warm brown eyes were pleading, though he said not a word. The sight gutted Connor. Jake bumped his shoulder again, reminding him of the stakes.

Connor bit down on his lip.

He had to think of something to trade. "We were waiting for a message from you about the baby," Connor stalled. "We were willing to negotiate to get the child back. But you never contacted us."

"That's because you don't understand what our purposes are for my daughter, and for my granddaughter." And with no further warning, Pim Wat lopped off Thom Tang's head.

Blood from the pilot's severed neck sprayed Connor in a hot, coppery-smelling spatter. Connor convulsed with a cry, falling to the ground. He heaved, emptying his belly. He writhed and fought, unable to silence his own rough cries of grief and horror as the ninjas grabbed him, dragging him and Jake toward the ATV.

Pim Wat was taking them back to the stronghold.

Yes, he'd made a grave error in coming on this mission.

CHAPTER FOURTEEN

Day Twenty-Four

SOPHIE SQUATTED UNDER THE BARBELL, then lifted with a powerful push of her glutes and legs. This exercise had been really hard to do even without weight when she first started; her entire pelvic area had been weakened by pregnancy and giving birth. Two weeks of steadily increasing weight and reps had brought her to an approximation of her former strength, and that wasn't the only change.

She'd lost the puffy water weight of pregnancy, her abs had tightened up a good deal, breast milk was down to almost nothing, and her chest was normal size again.

But as she did another set of squats, watching herself in the mirror, the ache of the Momi-shaped hole in Sophie's heart had not shrunk at all.

Today made two weeks since the men had left. Connor had communicated briefly at first, just a few short lines that came into the secret chat box they'd used to communicate since their first encounters online. He'd posted their progress: landing on the mainland, rendezvous with their team, the arrival at the surveillance node close to the stronghold, planting the cameras inside the fortress . . . then nothing.

Nothing! For a week.

Sophie dropped the bar and stomped over to the lat pulldown machine. She sat on the bench and used her abs for leverage as she pulled down on the bar, worry and anger a potent fuel.

She finished her weight routine and stood up, looking around the immaculate, top-of-the-line gym. Connor spared no expense on his equipment, and with Nam cooking healthy, nutritious food for her, she'd been in the equivalent of a fitness spa since her arrival.

Time for her afternoon run.

Sophie put in her earbuds and picked up her phone, checking it for the hundredth time for anything new. No ransom note or request had come in since the baby had disappeared. Alika had told her that the Kaua`i police had no further leads, and he'd updated Detective Jenkins recently on what Security Solutions was doing, operating on the assumption that Momi had been taken by her grandmother.

She'd caught up her father, Marcella, and her friend Lei, briefing them on the situation, but talking about it just made her angry and frustrated. After the initial calls, she'd stopped communicating except to let them know things were status quo.

As she thumbed to her favorite running playlist, the phone dinged with an incoming text message from an unknown number. She read: *"Sophie. This is Armita. Come to the magnolia tree to find what you seek."*

"What?" Sophie cried aloud. "What are you talking about?" She replied quickly: *"Tell me something only Armita would know so that I can be sure it's you."*

"Your dogs were beautiful the night I visited your balcony," came back immediately. *"Contact no one. I have left the compound with your treasure and she must not find us."*

Armita had to be referring to Pim Wat! And the magnolia tree? Where was that? *"What's going on?"* Sophie texted. *"Please, I need to know more!"*

"She will be looking for us. Come alone. Tell no one, not even your men."

A photo appeared on Sophie's phone.

Sophie gasped, her hand coming up to cover her mouth as she gazed down at her baby's photo—Sophie would know that precious face anywhere. Momi's large, light brown eyes were open. Angelic curls topped her head, and her cheeks were sweetly pink, and plump with health.

"Thank you, Armita. I will come," she texted back.

A message appeared: *Not Deliverable.*

Armita had destroyed the phone already. The nanny was taking no chances in being tracked.

Sophie sat down on the weight bench abruptly as her knees gave way.

She stared at her daughter's face, eating up the precious vision—and realized that the baby's head rested on a current newspaper, printed in Thai. The date appeared beside her tiny, shell-like ear.

Come alone and tell no one? What if the message was a trap?

The message could be from someone trying to lure Sophie out of hiding. Perhaps her nanny had caved in to pressure from her mother and told Pim Wat, or someone else, about that midnight visit she'd made to Sophie's apartment.

Only one thing was certain: this person had access to her daughter—the photo gave proof of life. Whoever it was also had access to Armita, because only Armita knew the details of her nighttime visit to Sophie—*and about the magnolia tree.*

Sophie shut her eyes. Her surroundings went dim as she was transported back in time to her childhood home, a large wooden compound built on palisades near the Ping River. The magnolia tree she remembered grew up through a raised deck upon which she'd loved to play with her cousins as a child. Tall and robust, its spreading arms had provided shade and a place to climb. They'd even had a rope swing tied to one of its branches.

That house had been sold many years ago, shortly after her

parents' divorce and Sophie's departure for boarding school. She'd then met her father at various hotels over the years, and spent time with her mother at her Aunt Malee's house, right next door.

Her Aunt Malee was the only relative she had kept in touch with after she escaped her ex-husband Assan Ang and emigrated to the United States. Did she dare contact her? She was right next to Sophie's former home. She could check on what was going on over there.

But what if Malee's phone was tapped? If someone was looking for Sophie, her father and her aunt were both likely surveillance targets.

She couldn't risk it.

She had to get a message to Connor and Jake about this. Wherever they were in the mission, the Yām Khûmkạn stronghold was now the wrong target.

Momi wasn't there.

Sophie headed for the computer room.

CHAPTER FIFTEEN

Day Twenty-Five

JAKE LAY CURLED up on his side in the corner of the large, stone-walled room with a drain in the center of it. Water seeped from cold, rough walls; weak illumination from light penetrating a slit high near the ceiling barely lit the room. He was naked, and he folded his legs tighter against his chest to preserve body heat, pressing against his fellow prisoner's back for warmth.

They'd already tried to get each other loose, but the ninjas who took them had placed crude brass handcuffs on their wrists—and so far, there was no getting out of them.

Behind him, Connor shivered nonstop. They'd crossed the line a while ago from employer and employee to friends. Jake worried that Connor couldn't hold out against Pim Wat for much longer. Jake had trained for this kind of treatment. Hamilton, while brave, hadn't any such background.

Jake looked down at his rope-bound feet. He'd spent some hours working on getting loose by rubbing his ankles back and forth against a rough protrusion on the floor, but he'd only succeeded in abrading the damp skin around his ankles, and now yellowish ooze darkened the coconut fiber ropes binding him.

"This isn't good." Connor's teeth chattered as he spoke. The tropical climate outside the compound might as well not exist in this basement dungeon.

"She's not going to get what she wants, and she doesn't take disappointment well." Neither man used Pim Wat's name when they spoke of her.

"She won't kill you, man. You're too valuable as a hostage—the CEO of Security Solutions ought to be worth a few mil to the Yām Khûmkạn."

"We don't know that they want anything but Sophie and the baby."

"We can't tell her what we don't know. Sophie's safe. But the baby's gone. Someone double-crossed her. That much is clear from what she's said." Jake tried for a bantering tone. "You'll be fine, Mr. CEO."

"I don't think she cares at all about money," Connor said softly.

Pim Wat had been torturing him and Connor for days: taking turns, making each other watch. She'd played with electrodes and sandbagged their bodies. Yesterday, her ninjas had pummeled their feet with sticks. He was sure there was more unpleasantness ahead.

Jake shut his eyes, regret suffusing him as he ticked over the decisions leading up to now. *They should have taken longer to assess the situation.*

Waited for a ransom demand.

Got more men.

Anything but imagined they'd be able to sneak up on this fortress!

How long had the Yām Khûmkạn been aware of their presence? Connor had told Jake that he suspected that they had been following their movements the entire time, and had waited until they were close to the compound to take them, just for their own convenience —so they wouldn't have to walk as far through the jungle.

Jake shut his eyes, trying to close out the memories of the night-time attack that had resulted in their capture.

Screams and cries. Splattering entrails. Ripe and terrible smells. Sick sound of steel against bone. Blood spray hitting Jake, warm and damp. The wet thunk of good men's heads hitting the ground.

Pim Wat, a small black spider of a woman, wielding death without a flinch.

They may have been stupid about this op, but at least they'd left Sophie on Phi Ni.

Sophie was alive and free. Maybe she could somehow help them. But when would she know to sound an alarm, contact Bix? They'd agreed the op was for two weeks, and according to his mental count, that was up about now.

Jake felt the vibration of feet walking on the stones, and stiffened. He tried not to give in to nausea as the door rattled.

Pim Wat always asked the same thing: *Where is Sophie? Where has she taken the baby?*

Yep, someone had double-crossed her, and the woman was pissed.

Jake felt Connor's shivering increase as the key turned in the lock. His friend's body tightened, a plucked bowstring.

He had to keep Connor calm, keep his resolve strong. Sophie getting help was their only hope. He turned his head to speak to Connor over his shoulder. "Fighting it makes it worse. She won't kill you. You're worth too much as a hostage back in the States. Now me, on the other hand . . ." Jake chuckled grimly.

Jake couldn't see Connor's face, but there was no mistaking the note of alarm in the man's voice. "I can't let her kill you. Sophie needs you."

Jake had no response to that statement, so he made none—it had become clear to him that Connor cared about Sophie, perhaps as much as he did.

The wooden portal scraped open. The wizened little man who did the torturing stood in the doorway a moment, surveying the room.

"Hello, Igor. We're still here." Jake had to draw attention off of Connor, and taunting and calling the man Igor helped beat back the horror. "We're ready for today's fun."

Pim Wat, trailed by a couple of ninjas in the Yām Khûmkạn's signature black, stepped inside behind Igor. She pointed a lacquered nail at Jake. "Loverboy seems talkative. Let's start with him. No more beatings, as I said before. I want them pretty."

Jake couldn't help the tightening of his abs as two of the ninjas lifted him up off the floor, the restraints cutting into his flesh.

He couldn't cover himself. Couldn't protect himself. Couldn't do anything but endure whatever came next.

At least he knew how to handle this. Connor didn't have that training, and he was close to giving up the Phi Ni site, and possibly a good deal of Security Solutions information. Any of that could lead to Sophie and endanger the lives of their operatives and clients—and cripple a possible rescue attempt.

The ninjas plunked Jake down on a crude wooden chair near the drain hole in the center of the room. He grinned at Pim Wat. "Seems like you plan to give me a good workout today."

"Fetch the water vessel." Pim Wat told her minions. She gazed at Jake, her head tilted like a curious bird, then stepped forward. She dragged her pointy nail down Jake's chest, leaving a ragged scratch, and grabbed his junk. She gave a squeeze that doubled him over, gasping. "I plan to purge some of your attitude, Jake. I doubt you'll find it pleasant."

CHAPTER SIXTEEN

Day Twenty-Five

WIND TUGGED at Sophie's hair and light danced over the waves as she steered the sleek, heavy speedboat toward a distant horizon.

Sophie had gotten a late start on her departure by waiting another night, trying to get through to the men. Now, she checked the fuel gauge, her brows pulled together in concern. She had filled the Chris-Craft with all the gas she could find in the boathouse, and had stowed a separate can on board. Still, even before leaving Phi Ni, she'd wondered if there was enough fuel to take them the approximately hundred kilometers to the mainland.

As the powerful engine sputtered and died, she had her answer. *"Foul offspring of carrion birds!"*

Sophie left the steering area and fetched the spare tank of gas. The Chris-Craft could be gassed from an inside filler neck in the gunwale; Nam had gone over the speedboat's operating manual with Sophie before she'd departed, helping her pack it with weapons, ammo, money, a native woman's outfit, bedroll, and some limited foodstuffs.

Sophie wished she could take Anubis, Connor's Doberman. In the weeks of her physical rebuilding, he'd been a constant and faithful companion, and company of a sort. Though he could provide a measure of protection on her journey, she couldn't bring him. With his exotic looks, the dog would draw too much attention as they traveled.

Sophie emptied the last of the small gas can into the tank and took a heading with the electronic GPS, gazing out over the tossing sea toward a hazy horizon line. *Ugh, she was still so far away from shore!* The smell of gas was thick in her nostrils as she radioed in to Nam.

"Come in, Home Base. This is Pearl."

She spoke in Thai so as not to draw attention, and she'd chosen Momi's name as her handle. Every time she spoke it, that name reminded her of the urgency of her mission.

"This is Home Base." Nam's voice crackled through the handheld.

"Refueling with backup tank. May not make it to the destination today. Any word from the forward location?"

"No word."

Sophie's heart sank, a hollow sensation under her breastbone.

"Keep me posted. Pearl out." Sophie put away the radio.

She was beyond worried about Jake and Connor's mission. She had sent messages repeatedly but to no avail, and the two weeks had come and gone. There was nothing she could do besides alert Security Solutions VP, Kendall Bix, of the team's return date being missed. She'd given the current head of the company all she knew about the status of the current mission and the fact that the men should have returned to Phi Ni by now.

She opened the choke so that the influx of fuel could make its way through the lines, and fired up the ignition. The engine caught after just a few tries. Sophie checked her heading again, and pushed the throttle forward.

The Chris-Craft leapt up onto a plane, the ocean purling back from its bow within seconds. Though a weighty craft, its sleek lines created tremendous momentum once the boat was in motion. Sophie programmed the adjusted heading into the speedboat's guidance system, sat down in the pilot's chair, and fixed her eyes on the distant smudge of the horizon as she held the wheel steady.

Gazing through the windshield, Sophie saw a flying fish lift off the water, and soar beside her. Up ahead, a cloud trailed a rainbow— it was raining near the coast. Long rays of sunlight played over the waves like fool's gold, but the beauty brought her no pleasure.

The boat was a problem.

Assuming she was able to make it to the distant shore, where could Sophie stow such an expensive craft? She would need it to return to the island, and her journey to her family's former home was still going to be a long distance on foot if she couldn't figure out a ride. She needed to keep a low profile that would not attract the Yām Khûmkạn's attention—it was best to assume that they had eyes and ears everywhere. The boat would certainly be attention-getting.

Sophie ran out of gas several kilometers short of the coast. *"Foul demon spawn!"* The speedboat wallowed in rolling waves as the sky changed from blue to indigo, and the dying day cast red beams over her shoulder.

She picked up a pair of binoculars and scanned the coast. Though tantalizingly near, the mainland was still too far away for her to attempt to swim in the waning evening light. She could too easily lose her way once in the water—not to mention encountering electric eels, sharks, or box jellyfish, hazards of these waters.

She had to find another way.

Sophie turned three hundred and sixty degrees, scanning the horizon with the binoculars. She spotted a nearby atoll to the east. One of the many outcrops off of the coast, this one appeared to be downwind. The Chris-Craft was already floating toward it, propelled by the light evening breeze.

Sophie opened the closed bench at the stern, looking for anything to help get her the remaining distance, and was delighted to discover a small electric trolling motor.

Sophie eyed the main coastline again. Still too far away, given the challenges of wind and time. But perhaps, in the morning, if the wind cooperated, she could make it to shore with the trolling motor. She'd worry about where to hide the boat to begin her overland journey once she got there.

Sophie dropped the trolling motor off the stern of the Chris-Craft and tightened down its clamps, attaching it to a narrow lip on the gunwale. She checked that the mechanism was hooked up to its accompanying battery, and turned it on with a switch on the side.

Forty-five excruciatingly slow minutes later, Sophie nudged the sleek bow of the speedboat into a tiny, sheltered bay between jagged arms of rock. She hurried to the bow, put out a rubber bumper guard, and tossed a loop of bow line over a boulder. She then cranked the rope tight around the cleat. The Chris-Craft squeaked as it rubbed against its rocky mooring, secured.

The light of sunset flamed across the back of the craft not in shadow as Sophie descended into the tidy cabin in the bow. There was no point in exploring the atoll; she had work to do, and this stop was a mere pause point.

Sophie got out her laptop and pulled up saved photographic maps of the area. She studied her route: hopefully, she would land near a fishing village and be able to make her way up a small dirt road to a more major thoroughfare that led toward Bangkok and the Ping River. Once on that road, Sophie could likely hire someone to drive her the rest of the way.

The route looked deceptively easy. "I hope it actually will be," she said aloud, missing the company of her Lab, Ginger, who'd provided companionship and an excuse to talk to herself when alone. Ginger, and Jake's dog Tank, were probably being spoiled by Alika and his family. That reminded her that she was overdue for updating Alika. As Momi's father, he deserved to know things had shifted.

Sophie took out the satellite phone she'd kept turned off with the battery removed, and reassembled it. She sent Alika a text that she had a lead on Momi, and hoped to know more soon.

Sophie fixed a simple meal of dehydrated food and ate it mechanically even as her belly cramped with anxiety. Her mind ground over what had happened to Jake and Connor, and what was going on with her precious daughter. What could have happened to the men, preventing them from communicating or returning? What more could she do to help?

And who was caring for Momi? Was she healthy? Given proper nutrition? Held and loved? Would she be emotionally or physically damaged by being kidnapped, as Sophie had been?

No. Momi would be fine. She was too little to remember any of this, and Sophie was betting her life that Armita was caring for her with love. They'd be reunited soon.

But the men? There had to be more she could do. An idea burst across Sophie's brain: *CIA Agent Devin McDonald.*

Sophie and Connor had been working with the agent on a plan for Sophie to become a confidential asset for the spy agency, reporting on the activities of the Yām Khûmkạn, as her mother drew her deeper into involvement with the clandestine organization. That plan had been put on hold when Sophie discovered she was pregnant. Sophie had informed the agent she was no longer interested in their proposal and was severing ties with her mother for the foreseeable future—she'd instinctively known Pim Wat was dangerous to her child, and how right she'd been!

The jowly CIA agent had reluctantly accepted her dictum, but told Sophie, "Keep in touch. Things can turn on a dime in this business, and you may well want our help or vice versa."

"Turn on a dime" was a new saying to Sophie, but it made sense —and things had, indeed, spun in a new direction—and maybe McDonald could do something to find out what had happened to Jake and Connor.

She called McDonald's number, routing through an untraceable scrambler site that connected via satellite. She and Connor had tried to use this method to keep in touch, but the jungle terrain had provided too much interference. Out here on the open ocean, she connected with his secure voicemail almost immediately.

"Agent McDonald, this is Sophie Smithson." She released a trembling breath, rubbing the scar on her cheekbone and organizing her thoughts. "A lot has happened since we last spoke. I don't know when I will actually be able to connect with you again, so I need to give you some urgent information. Sheldon Hamilton, CEO of Security Solutions, my partner Jake Dunn, and a party of seven trained mercenaries from our company have all disappeared from communication while trying to penetrate the base of the Yām Khûmkạn in Thailand." She gave as many details as she could about the mission. "I am headed to meet someone else who has provided proof of life of my child, and I'll be off the grid while I pursue this lead. But if you could investigate what happened to the rescue party, I would be . . . deeply indebted to the CIA." Sophie was basically signing up to work for them with this message, but who cared? *If the agency could do anything to find out what had happened to Jake and Connor, and potentially get them back, it was worth it.* "Please try me back at this number and leave a message."

She ended the call and stared down at the clunky phone in her hand.

She was out of ideas at the moment. Once she had Momi secured, she could come up with other plans. Despite her worries, she had to rest now. She would need all of her physical, mental, and emotional resources to deal with tomorrow.

Sophie disassembled the phone and closed down all of the visible light into the cabin as soon as the sunset had finished its annoying pageant. She took her antidepressant and a holistic sleep aid. She lay down on the cabin's bunk and shut her eyes.

Maybe there was a divine entity who could help when she'd reached the end of what she could do. "Divine Force in the universe, please protect my dear ones, especially Momi, Connor, and Jake. Help me know what to do at each stage of this journey—speak to me through insight and intuition, and show me which way to go and what to do. Help me save them. And tonight, give me sleep so I can be strong for tomorrow."

Sophie shut her eyes, and willed herself to sleep as she'd learned to do under Assan Ang's cruel hand.

CHAPTER SEVENTEEN

Day Twenty-Five

JAKE BEGAN BREATHING SLOW, deep breaths as Igor and Pim Wat's minions fetched the water vessel. He filled his lungs to capacity, oxygenating his blood, keeping his eyes closed and body consciously relaxed.

Pim Wat wouldn't know that he'd almost been a SEAL, but had gone with the Green Berets instead; she wouldn't know that he loved free diving and could hold his breath for close to five minutes, up to seven in a pinch.

Not that any of that mattered. Igor would keep going until Jake sucked water and thought he would die.

But the sensation of drowning was familiar, and the truth was, he wasn't afraid of dying. He was only afraid that he'd never see the woman he loved or his child again; that harm could still come to them.

He had to keep that from happening.

The men set the water vessel down, a big metal tub that likely had some other, mundane purpose, like doing laundry. *Maybe washing babies.*

Jake pushed fear away with powerful memories: Momi's newborn, vulnerable little form, the baby's kitten-like cries melting his heart, as she first entered the world. He and Alika had helped under the midwife's direction: cleaning up and cutting the cord, wrapping Momi up tight, and watching as Sophie put her baby to the breast for the first time.

He'd been there for Momi's first minutes of life. Reveled in the whole intense experience of her birth. Nothing could take that from him.

Dirty water, greenish and filled with sticks and leaves, splashed into the tub from buckets the ninjas dumped into it.

Jake couldn't hold onto the memory as the tub filled.

"How can I get a message to Sophie?" Pim Wat lifted Jake's chin, forcing his eyes up to meet large brown ones that were eerily like Sophie's. "I need to speak to my daughter."

This was a new question. Until now, she'd just repeatedly asked where Sophie was.

"Sophie was not involved with this mission. We came to get the baby back." Jake's heart beat with slow, heavy thumps as he continued to breathe deeply. Pim Wat could not reach Sophie with the news that they were captive. Sophie might give in to her mother's demands and trade herself for them. He and Connor still didn't know what Pim Wat really wanted with Sophie and Momi, but it couldn't just be simple family fealty. "We left her in Hawaii, recovering from the birth."

Pim Wat's eyes narrowed. A smile ticked up the corners of her full mouth. "The first information you actually give up, Jake, and it's a lie. Why am I not surprised?" She gave Igor a head nod.

Jake sucked a final breath as ninjas, positioned at each of his shoulders, shoved him forward and down. His face splashed into the dirty water. Igor's hand on the back of his head held him under.

Jake began a count. Leisurely, slowly. He would go to a hundred. After he got there, he'd go to another hundred. The process of counting kept him calm and distracted; he would not waste effort and oxygen struggling.

One alligator, two alligator, three alligator. . .

He got to three hundred. Igor pulled him up when he began to struggle.

Pim Wat's brows were scrunched with annoyance—clearly, she'd had to wait longer than she'd wanted to. "How do I reach Sophie? I just want to get her a message. No harm will come to her, I promise. She is my daughter, and you are her lover. Do you think I want her angry with me for killing her boyfriend? Please. Just give me a way to contact her." Those familiar brown eyes shone with sincerity.

Tempting. *Oh, it was so tempting.* Just give Sophie's phone number to end the suffering? He could buy time, give a fake one . . . Pim Wat was Sophie's mother. Surely, she wouldn't harm Sophie?

No. He could not give in. This woman was evil. She'd stolen Sophie's child. She had no good in mind for either of them.

Shivers passed over Jake. His bowels felt suspiciously loose. He had fought hard for that count to three hundred. He wasn't sure he had it in him for more. Somehow, he'd have to find that strength.

A movement drew Jake's gaze toward his companion.

Connor had rolled over to face them and got himself up onto his knees, though his feet were bound and wrists shackled behind his back. The man's glasses had been knocked off in the capture. Oddly, one of Connor's eyes was blue, and the other one brown.

What the hell? Why did the guy wear brown contacts? And why did he look so familiar, all of a sudden? He reminded Jake of someone . . .

"Stop. Please." Connor's jaw was tight; his mouth pinched. Yeah, it was no fun watching a buddy get tortured—but he couldn't let Connor crack. Jake gave his friend a slow wink as he sucked deep breaths, re-oxygenating.

"Do you care to intervene, Mr. Hamilton?" Pim Wat addressed Connor. "Want to answer my question and end your friend's diffi-culties?"

Jake shook his head behind Pim Wat's back, narrowing his eyes and mouthing "No." Igor must have seen because he grabbed Jake's hair and yanked his head back to hold him immobile.

Thankfully, Connor shook his head.

The ninjas and Igor plunged Jake under again. He began his count, but the burn in his chest was immediate. His body was starved for oxygen. *Not good.*

Overhead, through the water, he heard voices arguing. He couldn't make out the words. *Was Connor giving in?* Anxiety made Jake aware of the growing heat in his lungs, of the way his extremities were beginning to twitch and tremble. *Eighty-nine alligator, ninety alligator, ninety-one alligator . . .*

His head was yanked out of the water. A fist rammed into his solar plexus, blasting out his remaining air. He didn't have time to breathe again before he was thrust under once more. His body went into shock from the pain and loss of air, and his solar plexus expanded in a reflexive gasp. Water filled his throat and lungs with liquid fire.

Something no one tells you is that drowning really hurts. Ocean water, river water, pool water, toilet water—it all burns like acid going down, then smothers you like a fucking anvil on your chest.

But he wasn't going to die like this, drowned like a rat in a tub by these assholes. No way.

Jake got his bound feet underneath him and heaved up with all of his remaining strength, throwing his body backward.

The ninjas couldn't quite hold him—that's what happened when a two-hundred-pound, six-foot-two man fought for his life against a couple of hundred-and fifty-pounders. Jake got his face clear and tried to suck a breath, but his lungs were too full of water for it to work. Igor threw himself bodily on top of Jake's head, and down he went again.

Red spots. Roiling water. Blows and pain. The roar of his laboring heart.

Memories lit his brain in lightning flashes: *running with his sisters in a wheat field toward the sound of the ice cream truck. Happiness.*

Dropping in a parachute over Cambodia—the rush, a sense of wonder at the beauty of the world.

Sophie's face, her eyes closed, her lips parting for his kiss.
BLACK.

CHAPTER EIGHTEEN

Day Twenty-Six

DAWN WAS BARELY a pewter glimmer on the silky black ocean when Sophie woke. She fixed herself a cup of strong tea, ate a tasteless but necessary protein bar, and went topside.

She reassembled the satellite phone and checked for messages: *nothing.*

"Damn that spawn of a two-headed goat!" McDonald was likely in a bureaucratic meeting discussing her phone call. The CIA didn't move quickly on something like this.

Sophie had charged the electric motor on the boat's battery, but she still had to decide whether to try to swim to shore and leave the vessel safely anchored on the atoll, or try to get the Chris-Craft all the way to the coast on the electric motor's charge.

She had a judgment call to make, but first, she'd contact Nam and check in. "Home Base, this is Pearl. Any news?"

The radio crackled. She called again, but Nam did not respond.

Had the island fortress been discovered? Or was Nam just away from the radio, doing his usual morning routine?

No way to know. And now she had to decide.

Sophie assembled her backpack of supplies first, to assess how much she'd need to move through the water if she chose that route.

The backpack was significant—at least thirty pounds of camping equipment and water. Staring at it, Sophie sat back on her heels, still torn. That damn electric motor was sure to give out before it was able to get the heavy speedboat to shore, and she was too familiar with the hazards of this ocean to feel comfortable just jumping in with a backpack and a pair of swim fins.

Was there anything she'd overlooked? What if the Chris-Craft had some kind of emergency inflatable? Or even a blow-up mattress she could use for more flotation?

Sophie began a serious search of the boat, going through every cupboard and bulkhead—and sure enough, in a far forward hatch she hadn't noticed before, Sophie found a small, tightly rolled rubber dinghy. Less than six feet in length, with a flimsy collapsible paddle, the inflatable was not built for anything but a worst-case scenario. *It was perfect.*

Sophie unrolled it and discovered an emergency kit, complete with a water reclamation device, flares, a first aid kit, and an emergency beacon. "That makes me feel better," she said aloud, missing Ginger again with a sharp pang. And Jake? Connor? Her heart thudded with anxiety. Sweat broke out on her hands. "They're probably fine. Everything is fine. All you have to do is this, right now, Sophie—getting Momi back is the priority," she told herself aloud.

She hooked up the pump she uncovered beneath the inflatable, and soon she had the tiny, bright yellow craft blown up.

Sophie put it into the water, tying it to the Chris-Craft with a built-in cord. She loaded the heavy backpack into the raft. The lifeboat bobbed and tipped alarmingly, even in the gentle waves lapping their hidden berth.

Sophie frowned. Paddling that thing against wind and waves was going to be challenging if she couldn't find a way to hook up the small electric motor to the boat's squishy stern. And what if she lost sight of the land? She was no sailor; this whole thing was a steep learning curve.

Perhaps getting a look at her destination would help with her nerves.

Sophie made sure everything was secure and then jumped onto the boulder she'd tied the speedboat to. A pair of binoculars and the handheld GPS tucked in her pockets, Sophie clambered up the steep side of the atoll to get a look at the shore. The exertion of climbing, grasping the weathered rock and hauling herself ever higher, calmed her down. By the time she reached the stone atoll's apex, she was flushed with exercise and ready for anything.

Sophie took another heading from the peak, clinging to a scruffy, salt-burned bush, and locked in the coordinates. Even if she lost sight of the horizon, she just needed to keep going toward the direction she'd chosen.

Resolved, Sophie clambered back down.

She got into the life raft, just to get a feel for it. Yes, it was tippy, but if she sat in the middle and kept weight in the center, it settled. She wrestled the electric motor and its battery over the side and into the raft, and spent another half hour messing with it until she'd pinched enough of the rubber body into the motor's clamp to secure it to the raft's stern.

She closed and locked the Chris-Craft and hid the key, tying it in a sealed plastic bag to the rubber bumper against the hull—she couldn't take the chance of losing it before she was able to return.

And then, her heart drumming in her chest and her palms damp with sweat, Sophie slipped on a lifejacket, climbed carefully into the dinghy, and cast off.

CHAPTER NINETEEN

Day Twenty-Five

"Stop! Let him go!" Connor thrashed against his bonds, screaming, as he watched the torturer and his ninjas drown Jake in a tub of water. "I told you I'd tell you what you want!" His own heart seemed about to burst from the stress of watching Jake's dying struggle.

Pim Wat, standing to one side with her arms crossed, lifted her chin.

The ninjas hoisted Jake's upper body out of the tub and tossed him off the chair. Jake landed with a wet thump on the stones, falling onto his side.

Jake's face was blue, his eyes were closed, and water dribbled out of his slack mouth.

He wasn't moving at all.

"If he's dead I'm not telling you shit," Connor choked. "Not one fucking word."

"Oh, you'll tell me whatever I want to know. And a lot more besides, Mr. Hamilton." Pim Wat smiled. "I don't need Jake when I've got you."

"Resuscitate him, you bitch," Connor ground out. He crawled

forward on his knees, tugging at the shackles on his arms reflexively, frantic to reach his friend. Because that's what they'd become in this test of every human limit: *friends*. Brothers, who loved the same woman and were united in one purpose: keeping her safe, finding her baby, and surviving this impossible situation. *Maybe he could do mouth to mouth.* "You want me to talk? Help him. I'll die before I tell you anything if he's gone."

"What is this, Beautiful One?" A dark and silky voice, speaking in Thai, came from the door.

"Master." Pim Wat started and spun to face the room's opening. "Master, I am getting these men to give us the information we want."

Connor finally reached Jake. Using his head, he pushed Jake onto his back and leaned over to press his mouth against Jake's, blowing into his friend's cold lips. He emptied his lungs, then moved to the man's chest and banged his head down on it, ignoring the pain in his forehead as he counted out loud: "One, two, three, four, five."

He sidled back up to Jake's face, heedless of his bleeding knees. Foamy liquid frothed out of Jake's mouth—*was that good?* Maybe the water was coming out. He blew into Jake's mouth again with determination, emptying his lungs.

Rapid Thai flew over his head between Pim Wat and the Master, too quick for Connor's limited language skills to follow—an argument, to judge by the tone.

Pim Wat huffed angrily and left the room. Connor felt rather than saw her go, darkness lifting from the area as if a carrion bird left a carcass.

Someone was beside him, barking orders. The man Pim Wat called Master turned Jake on his side again, thumping his back hard. Water gushed from Jake's mouth. The Master lowered him down and began doing chest compressions. He and Connor counted aloud, synchronizing their efforts; between compressions, Connor breathed into Jake's foamy mouth. The Master lifted and turned him; more water flowed out as the Master hit Jake's back with heavy, open-handed blows.

Ninjas ran in with an external defibrillator and pulled Jake up and away from the puddle of water surrounding his body. The Master gestured for Connor to retreat. Connor shuffled out of the way as they applied the paddles to Jake's massive chest.

His friend's big body arched up, thumped down.

They did it again. Arch and thump.

"Come on Jake, come on, come on," Connor muttered. "Come back, dammit, we need you. *She needs you.*"

A third time.

Jake was still not breathing. His body remained slack and unresponsive.

The Master sat back on his heels and shook his head.

Connor shuffled forward and laid his ear on Jake's chest.

The faintest of thumps. He blew another breath into Jake's mouth, and this time felt the warmth of his friend's lips, the flush of his skin. "He's alive!"

The Master rolled Jake onto his side again and thumped his back some more. More foam emerged from his mouth, and Jake coughed and choked, breathing at last.

Connor sat back on his heels in relief. He wiped tears off his face onto his shoulder, laughing weakly. "You're a tough son of a bitch, Jake. Gave me a heart attack, man."

The Master barked something to the ninjas. Both of the men's restraints were removed. The Master covered Jake with a blanket the men brought in and kept him propped on his side as Jake continued to retch and cough, clearing his lungs.

Connor twisted his raw wrists, getting circulation back into his arms and hands. He rose slowly to his feet, feeling every scrape and bruise on his abused body. Cold drafting through the door lifted the hairs on his bare skin, and he covered his genitals instinctively. Jake appeared to be breathing more easily, and the Master looked up at Connor. "You need a bath. Clothing."

The Master's English was British-accented and clear, like

Sophie's. *He'd been foreign-educated.* He had strangely compelling dark purple eyes.

"You didn't know what she was doing to us?" Connor asked. "Pim Wat?" He hated to speak her name.

The Master didn't answer. He tucked a bit of blanket beneath Jake's head to pad the stone as he lowered the man back down. He barked more orders in Thai, and several ninjas brought additional blankets and carefully moved Jake onto one of them. They covered him with a clean one. Then, they lifted Jake and carried him out of the room.

The Master stood. He was tall for a Thai, and moved with a lithe grace that belied years hinted at by lines beside his eyes and a peppering of silver in long braided hair. He gestured to Connor. "Come with me."

Connor trailed him into the stone-lined hall, but the men carrying Jake were headed in the opposite direction. Connor stopped, looking after his friend.

"They're taking him to the infirmary. He will be cared for." *That voice.* Such a potent combination of compassion and command. Connor followed the Master.

CHAPTER TWENTY

Day Twenty-Six

WIND HIT the little yellow dinghy the moment Sophie reached the opening of the atoll's inlet. The flimsy raft's bow lifted as waves slapped against it, spray immediately dousing Sophie from head to toe. She pulled down the ball cap she had found in the speedboat's cabin, squinting into the glare of the sun off the waves.

So much for being able to keep an eye on that distant shore! Instead, Sophie shielded the GPS device underneath her thin parka, and glanced at it periodically to make sure she was still headed in the right direction.

The battle against wind and waves seemed to take hours. Sophie's world narrowed down to the tiller of the electric motor in one hand, the GPS in the other, and keeping the raft steady.

The flimsy craft was not designed for anything but random floating, and had no real steering. The craft weaved from side to side as the waves pushed back, and without rudder or center hull, Sophie was unable to keep a straight course. She was still a good distance from land when the electric motor gave out.

No sense keeping deadweight on board; there would be no way to charge the battery when she reached the mainland.

Sophie unclamped the motor and let it slip overboard. She also dropped off the heavy, useless battery. Hopefully she could find a more seaworthy craft to get back to the speedboat in; there was no way she would risk this passage carrying a newborn baby.

Sophie extended the collapsible paddle, changed her position to forward in the bow of the tiny craft, and began paddling.

She was glad of all the hours she had spent in the gym over the last two weeks as she stroked deeply into the wind and waves. And stroked. And stroked.

Sophie could tell she was making headway only by checking the GPS with the wind against her—but she was slowly inching forward.

Her mind drifted to Momi as her body engaged in the mindless activity of forward movement.

The first time she had felt the baby kick was a sensation like a feather tickling her insides. She'd been at the Security Solutions office in Hilo that she shared with Jake, and she'd called him inside. Closing the office door, she took his hand in hers, slid up her shirt, and set his big warm palm on her slightly rounded abdomen. She enjoyed the feeling of his fingers against her flesh, the intimacy of their gaze into each other's eyes as he waited to see what this was about.

Then, that fluttering. This time it was more like tickling bubbles, like the fizz of champagne.

She would never forget the way Jake's dawn-gray eyes seemed to light with infectious joy, his grin taking up most of his face. "Our baby is really in there!"

Sophie turned her head to wipe tears from the stinging spray on her shoulder. *He had to be alive; he just had to.*

And Connor?

She couldn't imagine her life without the man who had been her first lover since she'd escaped Assan Ang. Though he'd betrayed her in the cruelest way by faking his death to dodge the authorities, he'd worked hard and sacrificially to make up for it. He was the only person besides Dr. Wilson, her therapist, who knew all of her secrets and shared her passion for the wired world. Connor was more than a friend, and always would be.

Sophie finally reached the coast, and her laboring heart sank as she faced an impenetrable-looking mangrove swamp. She grasped onto a tree with wide, buttressing roots that dug deep into the silty bottom, and tied the dinghy to one of the roots for a moment so she could assess the situation.

The mangrove jungle was alive with sound; the squawks of kingfishers, the chatter of an egret, the chirps of plovers. The mangroves themselves creaked and groaned, their bark rubbing against each other as if in conversation. And everywhere, filling Sophie's nostrils, the thick, fecund smell of rotting vegetation.

After drinking some water and eating a restorative energy bar, Sophie took out the GPS again. This time she used a satellite map program to get an aerial view, and determined that the mangrove swamp probably extended no more than a mile inland.

She put the paddle outside of the dinghy to take a depth reading. The murky water was only a couple of feet deep—but that couple of feet would be home to many snakes, crabs, and other waterborne hazards. Sophie checked that the wet/dry hiking shoes she had donned were strapped on carefully, and she stuck a leg out of the raft.

Simple things, like climbing out of the dinghy without capsizing, were taking up way too much time and energy. Sophie suppressed a stab of worry.

Armita had not given her a deadline for their meetup. She would know that Sophie's journey, alone as specified, and trying not to be detected by the Yām Khûmkạn, might be difficult and hazardous—though she'd have no idea that Sophie had lost all of her backup. Haste was not going to help Sophie get to Armita faster; in fact, it might cause her to make the kind of mistake that could get her killed.

Up to her knees in brackish water, her feet sunk into a muddy silt bottom, Sophie took the flare gun and the first aid kit out of the dinghy and stowed them in her backpack. She took time to deflate and wrap up the raft, and walked into the trees, carrying the crudely rolled inflatable. Once deep enough into the mangroves not to be visible from the ocean side, Sophie stowed the raft and its collapsible paddle in the branches of one of the mangroves. She put a pin in the GPS. Worst-case scenario, if she had to reuse the flimsy craft, she could find it again.

Though carrying Momi? How could she paddle? Maybe a sling to keep the baby close . . . and hopefully the wind would be at her back. It seemed way too dangerous to use the raft again, but she would do whatever she had to, to get her child home.

Tightening down the straps of the backpack, Sophie forged deeper, the GPS in her hand as she navigated the tangled roots of the mangroves. She kept her eyes moving and her arms and legs as far away from the reaching branches and roots as she could.

A great heron flapped up in a whirl of wings, startling Sophie, and she fell back against one of the mangroves. She shrieked as she landed on something moving. She recoiled, almost losing her grip on the GPS as she jumped away—only to see a harmless four-foot python withdraw higher into the branches of the tree.

Sophie calmed herself with an effort, refocusing and taking another reading on her direction using the GPS. *It would not be good to get lost in here.* The mangroves were a maze, their spreading roots creating little islands, and often so close together that there was no way to pass between them. This forced Sophie to keep moving laterally to wherever she could find a way through, and without a GPS to give her a direction, she would soon have been hopelessly lost.

Stories of people wandering or snakebitten in the mangroves, starving and dying only meters from well-trafficked areas, were the stuff of urban legend in Thailand.

She pushed on, only stopping when she felt a vicious pinch on her foot, all the way through her hiking shoe. She kicked wildly, and a large, blue-tinged crab flew out of the water to hit one of the trees. Her kick detached it forcibly from her toe. On another day she might have laughed; today it was one more threat knocked down, nothing more.

Sophie took deliberate calming breaths, her eyes scanning the thick growth around her for any of the multitudinous types of tree snakes or large, stinging insects. She moved even faster, swishing through the water as quickly as she dared.

Once again, the journey seemed to take forever, but it couldn't have been more than a couple of hours when Sophie grasped onto a mangrove's wet roots and hauled herself out of the water onto a slippery mud bank. Checking her heading, she pushed forward through heavy brush toward a thin line on the screen showing some kind of track.

Sophie tried to remember her early years in Thailand, but the truth was, she had never spent time in the wilderness; she'd always stayed close to home at the family compound near Bangkok. She didn't remember ever having come this far out into the countryside. The idea of bushwhacking through virgin jungle, alone, would never have occurred to her family with anything but horror.

The muddy bank gave way to waist-high grasses interspersed with tropical trees. Sophie ate another energy bar, supplemented by a couple of guavas. The food gave her enough energy to pick up her pace to a trot once she found a narrow cow path.

She kept a close eye out for the area's worst hazard, the monocled cobra. Cobras liked grassy areas, and this type of field was their favorite kind of habitat. Mostly feeding on rats and mice, cobras were aggressive when frightened—and the last thing Sophie needed to deal with right now was an extremely venomous snakebite.

The baaing of animals ahead speeded her on—*where there were domestic animals, there were people!* A few hundred yards farther, Sophie felt her spirits lift to spot a native farmer dressed in simple clothing tending a herd of goats. She greeted him in Thai with a grateful smile and a small bow, ignoring his astonished expression at her unexpected appearance. "Can you direct me to the road? I am lost."

He did better than that, escorting her, along with his bleating charges, all the way to the dirt track she'd identified on the GPS. She thanked him and then dug into her pocket, producing a handful of colorful cash. "Can I hire you to take me to the outskirts of Bangkok?"

CHAPTER TWENTY-ONE

Day Twenty-Five

CONNOR FOLLOWED the Master down a dank, mildew-smelling hallway to a flight of cut stone stairs. His legs were still weak from being bound for days, and his belly was hollow—he was long past the point of mere hunger. He gritted his teeth and gripped the rough wall to help pull himself forward, but dizziness forced him to lean against it.

The Master turned to look at him, then without a word, looped Connor's arm over his shoulder and helped him up the stairs. At the next landing, he told the ninjas stationed there to take Connor to his chambers and prepare a bath. "Treat his injuries. I will be along to speak with him after he has had time to rest." Connor kept his head hanging, not letting on that he understood the language.

"Your chambers, master?" Disbelief was clear in the ninja's voice.

"You heard me the first time." The Master made a gesture with his hand. The man dropped to the ground and began doing push-ups.

Another ninja rushed forward to take Connor's weight. "Right away, Master."

Connor glanced back as he was half escorted, half carried down the hall. The Master had disappeared down the stairs again, but the ninja who had misspoken was still doing push-ups. Connor had the feeling that he would not stop until he collapsed. *How did the Master command such obedience, even from Pim Wat?*

Connor was borne along the hallway to a sumptuous apartment. The ninjas carrying him barked out orders to a guard standing by the door of the apartment, and that guard ran off as the ninja hoisted Connor through the doorway.

Connor lowered his head as if exhausted, which he was—but he also needed to take in and observe everything about this environment. *This could be his only chance to escape.*

Persian carpets and embroidered tapestries softened the harsh stone of the living area they entered, set with a low divan and a comfortable armchair arranged with a low table in front of a fireplace. A fire crackled on the hearth, rich with the smell of sandalwood. Priceless artworks, framed in gold, glowed from the walls.

Through one open door, Connor glimpsed a majestic bedchamber. And through another, a bare, monastic cell of a room with nothing to soften it but a small prayer rug, rolled out in front of a flickering brazier on an altar.

The master was allowing Connor to see inside not only the fortress of the Yām Khûmkạn, but his own private living space.

To what purpose? This whole situation could be an elaborate game of "good cop, bad cop" designed to gain his trust.

The ninja helping him assisted Connor into a bath chamber off of the bedroom. A stone privy with a polished wooden seat and cover hid behind a painted screen; a ewer of polished tin held water for rinsing away the waste. A huge copper bathtub dominated the room.

Connor parked himself on the privy while several ninjas carrying buckets filled the tub with steaming water.

So far, Pim Wat was the only woman he'd seen in the whole place.

Connor was nodding with exhaustion when the tub was finally filled and he was helped into warm, herb-scented water. He nearly fell asleep as his body was scrubbed and his wounds cleaned. Finally, the ninjas helped him out of the bath. They helped him onto a stone platform covered with layers of absorbent cotton cloth —a crude massage table, Connor realized, as an older ninja with kind eyes and a tonsure of hair around his baldpate entered the room.

The healer assessed Connor with gentle fingers, anointing his many bruises and scrapes—and finally, covered him with a blanket.

He slept.

PIM WAT GROUND her teeth as she stomped away from the holding cell. How could the Master undercut her like that before the men? Before the prisoners?

She powered up the rough stone stairs to her apartment and opened her mouth to shout for Armita—and remembered again a wound that tore into her heart. *That faithless jade had taken her granddaughter and disappeared!*

"*Foul daughter of the devil! Offal of a rotting goat!* How could you do this to me, Armita!" Pim Wat's eyes stung suspiciously. *No! She wouldn't cry over that miserable she-hag!*

Bursting with fury, Pim Wat stormed into the small antechamber that had been Armita's, opening off of her own apartment. She flung open the wooden cupboard that held Armita's clothing. Most of Armita's simple wardrobe was gone, but a few nicer gowns that Pim Wat had given her for public appearances and travel still hung neatly in the armoire.

Pim Wat pulled a knife from her waistband and slashed the garments, cursing and growling. No, she wouldn't cry over her maid's betrayal—but she would *rage.*

Rage was good. Rage protected her. Rage felt like cleansing fire.

And just that suddenly, the rage was spent, disintegrating into the empty ash of loss.

Pim Wat stood in a pile of brightly colored silk, satin, lace, and cotton, the narrow-bladed knife dangling from her hand. Rags still clung to a few hangers. Armita's personal scent, a gentle aroma of sandalwood and beeswax, rose from the ruined garments.

Grief and loneliness swamped Pim Wat.

She was alone. Betrayed by those closest to her. She'd devoted her life to the Master and to the Yām Khûmkạn; and what did she have to show for it? *Nothing!*

Her daughter was an angry, distant stranger. Her maid and closest friend had stolen her grandchild. And now her lover had betrayed her and embarrassed her in front of their men.

Worst of all was how keenly Pim Wat missed Armita. Her daughter's nanny had been with her seven days a week for more than twenty years.

Pim Wat fell to her knees in the midst of the shredded fabric. She let go of the knife, and scooped the ruined clothing into her arms. Crushing her face into the scraps, she gave way to her tears, weeping without restraint.

"Beautiful One." The Master's hand on her shoulder was a point of heat in a world gone cold. He dropped to kneel beside her, drawing her close. He kissed her forehead, wrapping her in his arms. "Haven't I told you that you must master your emotions?"

"I cannot," Pim Wat sobbed.

He pressed her wet face into his chest. She sagged, melting against him, and he tipped up her chin and kissed her. "I love the taste of your tears for how rare they are." He kissed her some more, lifted her out of the pile of ruined clothing, and carried her to the bed.

They had played many games on that bed—extended their pleasure with props and techniques, with role play and bondage and chemical assistance. But this time the Master merely stripped her and took her, and comforted her with his body and his love.

She cried again at the end, and he drank her tears.

He stroked her naked flesh as their passion cooled and they lay facing each other. "You did wrong with those men, Beautiful One. That violence was not what I wanted."

Pim Wat gazed into his eyes. Sated from passion, their color reminded her of deep purple pansies. "You gave me freedom in how to achieve the goal. I only sought to get the outcome we wanted."

"But you did not need to hurt anyone to get that. I want you to watch how I get what we want without even one more act of suffering."

Pim Wat frowned. "They are willing to die before they tell you anything."

"We will simply tell them the truth. They will communicate with your daughter, and she will come to us and give us what we want in exchange."

"I don't understand how that will happen." Pim Wat sat up and rubbed her eyes. "Sophie Malee hates me now."

"You have caused that, my Beautiful One. You do not understand people and what motivates them. Of her own free will, Sophie will come to us. And Hamilton? I have plans for him. He is more than he appears."

Pim Wat recognized the speculative look the Master got in his eye when he was considering a highly placed recruit. "You have a hundred apprentices," she snorted. "Hamilton is not malleable clay."

"You don't see in him what I do." The Master's face was calm, implacable. "He wants so much more from his life than he is getting. I can give that to him."

"I don't understand your interest in Hamilton. It's Jake who is her lover; you need him to get her to come. And I don't want to let Jake go." Pim Wat bit her lip, pouting.

"You killed him. Fortunately, Hamilton and I revived him."

"I didn't mean to kill him. I had other plans for Jake . . ." Pim Wat fiddled with a jade ornament tied into the Master's hair, averting her eyes.

"I know. You wanted to violate him. Make him serve you in bed. Hurt your daughter by forcing her lover."

Pim Wat looked up reluctantly. The Master saw Pim Wat clearly, but nothing in his demeanor changed; his eyes were still velvety and loving.

"You are a cobra, my Beautiful One. Hissing and venomous. But you are *my* cobra." He stroked her breast, tweaked her nipple. "My deadly love. I will satisfy your bloodthirsty urges." The Master wound his hand in the skein of her long black hair, pulled her closer so that she bared her throat to him. "You need no one but me. You want no one but me." But instead of her neck, he leaned over and bit her breast.

Pim Wat shrieked. She bit him back, sinking her teeth into his shoulder. They wrestled and thrashed; blood was drawn on both sides —and the Master thoroughly obliterated her lingering thirst for Jake's body.

CHAPTER TWENTY-TWO

Day Twenty-Five

"HAMILTON." *Someone was calling his name.*

Connor woke and groaned at the stiffness of his body. He looked up. Rosy sunset filtered through a narrow slit at the top of the room —the day was almost gone. He was chilled and sore; the bruises around his wrists and ankles throbbed.

"You will feel better once you have eaten." The Master's captivating voice came from the doorway. "Come. Join me for dinner."

Connor swung his legs off the stone platform and sat up, fighting dizziness. He slid down to stand, pulling the cloth that had been used as a towel off the stone and wrapping it around his naked waist before spotting a black gi hanging from a peg on the wall. He took a moment to don the shirt and loose pants, knotting the belt at his waist. He was stronger, and walked straighter—but now he felt a grinding pinch in his belly, the gnaw of urgent hunger.

A small round table had been set up in front of the fireplace, and the divan and loveseat moved back. One of the ninjas carried in a tray loaded with covered dishes, bowed to the Master, and left, closing the door behind him.

Connor eyed the table for anything like a weapon, but a pair of wooden chopsticks did not seem like a weapon that would make a dent on a martial artist of the Master's stature—because though he'd never seen the man in action, everything about him spoke of deadly competence.

A lamp burned on the rough stone wall, bathing the Master in a subtle glow as he used a simple bamboo scoop to serve a delicious-smelling meat and vegetable stir fry over rice into a bowl for each of them. He poured a ruby-colored drink from a carafe into horn cups. Connor watched as the man picked up his chopsticks. Every movement was graceful and definite.

"Eat. You must regain your strength," the Master said. "But not too fast."

Connor nodded and picked up his chopsticks. *Why was this man being kind to him?* Had he really not known what Pim Wat was up to in her torture chamber? Did he know how she'd executed his men in the jungle? Clearly this man was in charge—but Pim Wat must be a lieutenant or second in command.

The food was as good as it smelled—fresh and perfectly cooked, redolent of ginger, lemongrass, and garlic, and the rice fragrant and sticky. Connor found himself wolfing down the meal. He forced himself to slow down, to chew carefully, to quaff the ruby-colored drink, some kind of tangy fruit juice, between bites.

Suddenly full, he pushed his plate away, breathing through a wave of nausea.

The Master rang a small brass bell. The ninja who'd helped Connor cleared their plates, then returned with a tea tray. The man closed the outer door, leaving them alone.

"I know who you are," the Master said. He poured tea into translucent porcelain cups.

Connor's belly lurched—he *had* eaten too much. "I don't know what you mean." He took the delicate teacup, turned it in his hands, trying to warm his cold fingers.

"You are the computer vigilante called the Ghost."

Connor set the cup down too hard. Tea splashed onto the tray. "Ridiculous."

The Master sat back. A slight smile curled his full lips. "You needn't worry. I don't even plan to tell my Beautiful One, though how I found you was through tracking her phone communications. She's been receiving information from you for over a year now. Targets you want her to eliminate. And she has done that for you."

Connor lifted the teacup again, for something to do.

He'd taken out the remaining brown contact lens and dropped it as soon as he could after his wrists had been freed; the thing had been in his eye way too long and had irritated his cornea. He guessed that the brown hair dye was fading from his naturally blond locks too. His cover as Sheldon Hamilton was blown.

Had Jake gotten a good look at him with only one contact in? Hopefully not. If Jake ever put Connor's Sheldon Hamilton identity and the deceased Todd Remarkian persona together, he'd be pissed—at Connor, but even more, at Sophie for keeping Connor's secret.

"There's a reason I disguised my looks," Connor said. "But this vigilante stuff is nonsense." Deny, deny, deny.

"I won't engage in petty argument with you." The Master sipped his tea.

Connor looked around. "Where is the baby? We came for her."

"The child is no longer here." The Master set his cup back on the tray and laced his fingers over his flat belly. A fresh scratch marred the golden-brown skin of his neck; Connor could have sworn it hadn't been there when he'd seen the man earlier. "This is no place for a baby."

"Where is she?"

"That need not concern you. What should concern you is that we still need Sophie." The Master leaned forward, meeting Connor's eyes. "The Yām Khûmkạn's primary mission is to protect and serve Thailand's royal family. We are the remnant of the dynasty's original castle guard." The Master poured more tea. The aromatic scent settled Connor's roiling stomach. "The crown prince is only nine years old. He has a rare form of leukemia. Sophie is his second cousin, and out of all the world the only match that we've been able to find to donate needed bone marrow to him. We need her to save his life."

Connor's mouth had fallen open somewhere along the way, and he closed it with an effort. "Why didn't Pim Wat just tell Sophie this? Ask her to donate the marrow?"

"My Beautiful One . . . hates to admit any weakness. Appealing to her daughter's compassion is not her style."

"Stealing Sophie's child has not endeared her, either."

"Pim Wat claims taking the child was an impulse. She hoped the baby would be a match for the prince, and that she would not need to bring Sophie here since Sophie had proved recalcitrant. But the infant was not a match. Then, Pim Wat's maid took her and disappeared." The Master sipped his tea imperturbably.

Connor sat up as adrenaline hit his system. "Armita took the baby."

"Yes."

"And I take it you don't know where they are."

The Master's pansy-colored eyes met Connor's squarely. "Do you think you would even be alive right now if Pim Wat had the baby to use as leverage on Sophie?"

Connor's heart thudded. "You expect Sophie to come here and donate bone marrow in exchange for Jake and me?"

"Yes." The Master leaned forward. "And because she would not want to see an innocent child die. Her own relative."

Connor sat back and shook his head. "I'm guessing Armita is in touch with Sophie now. Sophie will stop at nothing to be reunited with her child. She won't come here once she has Momi. You've miscalculated."

"I don't miscalculate. She will come for you." They locked eyes. Connor looked away first. "Put your wrist on the table," the Master commanded.

Connor found himself doing so, resting his fist, fingers up, on the flat surface. Riverlike blue veins tracked over his rigid ligaments, disappearing into the meat of his muscled forearm. The insides of his wrists were marked by the brass handcuffs, purplish creases and red scrapes marring the pale skin.

The Master put his forefinger and middle finger on a spot just below Connor's hand. He pressed down lightly.

Connor froze, paralyzed. His breath caught and held—his diaphragm refused to respond. His body went rigid. He couldn't even blink. His skin crawled with bizarre sensations. There wasn't a thing he could do about any of it—he was trapped in his immobile body.

"There are secrets I can show you." The Master's voice was as potent as the strongest narcotic. "With your computer skills and my talents, we could topple governments. Make kings and queens. Raise fortunes, and crash them on the unworthy. Set free the Four Horsemen of the Apocalypse, if we so desire." Those bizarre purple eyes drilled into Connor's soul. "Think about it." The Master lifted his fingers, releasing him.

Connor breathed again. Blinked again. He yanked his arm up against his chest. Pushed his chair out. Stood up and backed away, all the way to the wall. "I can do all I want to with just my computer."

The Master smiled. "You've been frustrated many times by the vast world of people who don't keep a digital footprint. I can help with that." He flicked a crumb off his immaculate white *gi*. "Think about it. That is all I ask." He rang the brass bell and addressed the now familiar ninja servant. "Take this man to the barracks. I find I tire of his company."

The ninja tugged Connor away.

He was unnerved by how much he wished the Master would let him stay.

CHAPTER TWENTY-THREE

Days Twenty-Six and Twenty-Seven

JAKE LAPSED in and out of consciousness as he lay in the white-walled chamber that must be the compound's infirmary. Had he really just died, and been brought back? His body confirmed, with a multitude of pain, that was the case.

A kind-faced older man hooked him up to oxygen, treated his wounds, and surprised him by hooking up an IV. "Just getting you hydrated." The man had an Australian accent. "And a little something for the pain."

Jake floated away on a rosy cloud of meds, and fell asleep.

When he woke, his "belly was chewing on his spine," as his mama used to say, and the older ninja was right there beside his pallet, handing him a nourishing bowl of meat broth.

Jake was able to sit up and eat it himself.

Eating felt surreal. He was still, mentally, halfway wherever he'd gone when he died.

This brush with death was far from his first near miss, but it was his most serious.

Black.

That's all there had been.

No angel choir, no Grandma welcoming him from the other side, no favorite pup Shadow from his youth, begging for a pet. *Maybe there was no heaven.*

Naw. He refused to believe that. He just needed to be dead a little longer.

Jake spooned up the last of the soup and swallowed it. The heat and soft texture felt good on his raw throat.

He felt bruised, hammered on, wrecked. Like he'd gone ten rounds with Mike Tyson, and the dude had focused on his internal organs, specifically his lungs. It still hurt to breathe.

Why was he alive?

And . . . why did Connor have one blue eye, and one brown?

Connor had to have pleaded for his life. Maybe caved and offered Pim Wat what she wanted to hear. But hadn't there been another man there? Dressed in white, with the most unusual eyes . . .

Eyes haunted Jake as he drifted back to sleep.

Purple eyes. And Connor's eyes. One blue, one brown . . .

He woke abruptly.

The room was dim with early morning. Night must have passed.

He knew who Connor was.

Todd Remarkian. Sophie's first lover.

His brain had added up all the clues as he slept.

Remarkian had supposedly been Hamilton's business partner at Security Solutions. The blond, blue-eyed Aussie had been killed by a bomb close to two years ago. Remarkian had been Sophie's boyfriend—a man who would still be with her if he hadn't been "killed."

Only Remarkian wasn't really dead. He lived a double life, hiding behind colored contacts, dyed hair, and a pair of hipster glasses, masquerading as the CEO of their company, Sheldon Hamilton. And Sheldon Hamilton was also a man who called himself *Connor*, a man who loved Sophie as much as Jake did.

Todd/Sheldon/Connor. A man Jake had come to regard as a friend.

Jake lay rigid, his mind whirling. *Why had Remarkian faked his own death?*

He had to be the Ghost vigilante. There was no other reason the man would have set in motion such an elaborate ruse; nothing else made sense. The FBI had been onto him, so he'd faked the death of his Todd Remarkian persona, and kept his Hamilton identity.

Sophie had to know that her first lover was still alive.

The betrayal . . . Jake groaned aloud at the pain. His inarticulate cry bounced off the stones and mocked him.

He'd taken one blow after another from Sophie. *Had she ever been honest with him?* Told him the truth? Chosen him first, over others?

Was she really with Connor, or with him?

And let's not forget Alika, Momi's biological father, the "baby daddy." At least Jake was reasonably certain Sophie was over *that* guy!

"Son of a bitch," he muttered, covering his eyes with his hands. "Holy crap. Oh my God." No curses of any kind seemed adequate. Jake rolled on his side and groaned again, his eyes stinging.

Everything was sore, and there was no escape from his pain.

He punched the stone, because punching beat tears any frickin' day. He welcomed the pain of his split knuckles.

The door, a crude wooden affair, creaked open. Jake rolled over, shading his eyes from light pouring in.

The man with the purple eyes stood framed in it, staring down at him.

"How are you?" Purple Eyes had a British and Thai accent, and his voice was mellow and kind.

"Just dandy." Jake's throat felt like someone had taken a cheese grater to it, and it sounded about as good. "Nothing like dying in a tub of water to make you appreciate life."

Only he didn't appreciate life. He ought just to have died, rather than have to deal with this latest punch to the gut. He'd thought Connor was a friend, but never had the man so much as hinted at his other identity throughout all those long days they'd spent in close proximity.

Connor and Sophie had conspired against him. Kept him out of the loop. Who knew what their relationship really was? Jake shut his eyes, overwhelmed.

"Your friend cares for you very much," Purple Eyes said. "He saved your life."

"He's not my friend." Alarm flushed Jake's system. "What did he promise you?" *Connor had to have caved . . .*

"The crown prince of Thailand needs Sophie's help." Purple Eyes settled himself, resting a hip on the edge of Jake's low, wood-framed pallet. "The prince is dying of a rare form of leukemia. He needs a bone marrow transplant. Sophie is his only match."

Jake absorbed this. "Why didn't you—or Pim Wat—just tell us that? Ask Sophie to be a donor? After all, isn't the prince some kind of relative?"

"Second cousin." Purple Eyes stroked his chin thoughtfully. "I left it up to Pim Wat, thinking she was the one to approach her daughter. She seems to have made a mess of things."

"We couldn't figure out why Pim Wat wanted Sophie to come here so badly," Jake rasped. "And is that why Pim Wat snatched Sophie's baby?"

The man inclined his head in assent. "The baby is gone. The nanny stole her."

Jake's chest squeezed painfully. "What?"

"We don't know where Armita took the child." Purple Eyes shook his head. "I should have monitored the situation. Intervened sooner."

"What did Hamilton tell you?" He couldn't keep his voice casual. *If Connor gave up Sophie's location . . .* But he wouldn't. The guy loved Sophie too. Jake bit back another curse, remembering the betrayal afresh.

"Connor has said nothing. He is being treated well." Purple Eyes really had a magnificent voice; it reminded Jake of a cello, melodic and many-toned. "But soon he will tell me everything I want to know. Rest. You have nothing to fear." The man got up and left, closing the door and taking the light with him.

The kind-faced healer knocked, then entered with an herb-smelling bowl of water and a cloth. He laid a cool palm on Jake's brow. "How are you feeling?"

"Like I died, and there was no heaven," Jake said, and shut his eyes.

CHAPTER TWENTY-FOUR

Day Twenty-Six

SOPHIE CLIMBED down off the back of the full truck bed loaded with vegetables and crowded with loud, protesting goats corralled into a crude wooden enclosure. She was tired and sore, and smelled overwhelmingly of goat, but at last she was in Bangkok and within ten miles of her goal.

Sophie walked around to the front of the small Mitsubishi truck and handed the farmer a wad of bright Thai *baht*. *"Kóóp khùn káà.* Thank you. I will go find my family home now." Staying with a variation of the truth was always easiest; she'd claimed to be a lost tourist looking for her aunt's house.

Sophie hefted her backpack. She still had miles to go to find the family compound at the edge of the city, and dark was fast approaching. She needed to find a hotel to clean up and change in; somewhere with Wi-Fi so she could reconnect with the outside world.

Scooters and pedestrians swirled around Sophie as she navigated across an unpaved road, weaving in and out of the chaotic traffic. Sounds assaulted her: the wail of a child, the barking of dogs, the squealing of pigs being herded to market, and the ever-present honking of traffic with few rules to regulate it.

And the odors! Sophie wished she could pinch her nose against the reek of sewage, rotting fruit, and diesel fumes that colored the air.

She passed a tea stand and spent some *baht* on a spicy chai beverage. Sipping the tea, she pressed on down the busy thoroughfare, headed for the Western Thai Vacationer Hotel, an inn she'd researched ahead of time.

The area's buildings seemed to lean inward, pulled toward each other by thick powerline spiderwebs. Shops lined the street, and vendors called out and showed off their wares as she passed. Sophie avoided eye contact to try to keep them from approaching her, but her American clothes made her an easy target for sales pitches. Once inside the hotel's quaint but elegant space, Sophie breathed a sigh of relief.

She had forgotten that the country of her youth was so loud, intense, and colorfully beautiful.

She approached the front desk and requested a room, registering it under her Mary Watson identity.

Tomorrow, when she was fresh and clean, she would take a transport to the site of the magnolia tree. Tomorrow, she would know if this journey had been a fool's errand.

SOPHIE WOKE with a start in the pitch-dark room with its blackout drapes drawn. Her breasts ached and the front of her shirt was soaked.

She thought that she'd stopped lactating, but the dream she had had was so vivid . . .

Sophie shut her eyes, willing herself back into the dream.

Sophie and Momi were sharing a warm bath. The two of them were immersed in the tub, and Sophie cuddled and kissed her tiny girl, rinsing suds out of her child's curls. She blew a gentle raspberry on Momi's stomach, making the baby arch with the Moro reflex she had read about, the infant's legs folding tight to her abdomen. She hugged Momi close, snuggling her in against her wet naked skin, reveling in her daughter's velvety softness and sweet scent.

The warm bath felt as if they were swimming in amniotic fluid together with no separation; they were as physically and emotionally bonded as they could be. Momi nuzzled into Sophie's neck, seeking nourishment, and Sophie slid her downward and presented her nipple. Sophie felt the powerful sensation of her baby latching on as she nursed. The baby gazed up at Sophie, her golden-brown, long-lashed eyes serious. One tiny starfish hand reached toward her mother's face.

Tears pricked Sophie's eyes.

She flung the bedcovers off with a curse. This was no time for lounging around; her child needed her!

She had spent hours in the hotel room the night before, working through multiple VPNs to see if there was any news of the missing men. She'd put a communiqué out to McDonald at the CIA, and surfed online connections for any trace of news. She'd contacted Bix on Oahu, asking for an update. Security Solutions had notified Interpol and the authorities, but no response was forthcoming.

No one wanted to take on the Yām Khûmkạn on their home turf. *It was as if the men had fallen off the planet.*

Sophie fixed a tepid cup of tea in the room's coffeepot as her belly tightened with the memory of her online searching. There had been no contact from anyone to the house on Phi Ni.

Sophie had to let it go for now. She'd done all she could to put forces in motion to rescue the team. Now it was up to her to rescue her daughter.

Sophie opened her backpack and unrolled the native costume Nam had packed for her, accompanied by a Muslim headscarf with a translucent black veil that covered half her face.

She donned a long skirt with concealed split legs for movement along with a long-sleeved linen blouse. She draped the head covering over her short hair, secured the veil section of the headscarf, and gazed at herself in the mirror.

The garments were loose and concealing, better than any disguise. No one would question her with culture and modesty so clearly advertised. She was just a Muslim woman, similar to any other except for her height—at five foot nine, she still towered over most of the female population. But for the first time in a long time, Sophie felt invisible—and was grateful for the anonymity. Only her eyes and nose showed—and the wicked scar that ran up her cheekbone, past her eye, and into her hairline.

She turned to the pack and removed a small nylon drawstring bag for just her essentials. She would store the backpack here at the hotel for retrieval later. She called down to the desk and arranged that, and then checked out over the phone.

She sipped her tea, eyeing her unfamiliar appearance in the mirror.

What if this was a trap? A plan to lure her into Pim Wat's reach? What if Pim Wat had Momi, and had coerced Armita into bringing her here?

But why?

Nothing about this whole situation really made sense. She just had to move forward and hope for the best. "Just put one foot in front of the other," she said aloud. "That's what Marcella would tell me."

Thinking of her best friend reminded her of her father. She had kept him apprised during her time on Phi Ni with brief text messages every three days—but now she felt the need to hear his mellow voice. She reassembled the satellite phone and called his personal cell.

When he answered, relief broke over her in a wave. Sophie shut her eyes. "Hello, Dad."

"Sophie!" Francis Smithson's Morgan Freeman-like bass voice was not mellow today. "I've been going nuts with worry! What the hell is going on?"

She hadn't seen her father since before the birth; he'd planned to come to Kaua`i for that event, but she'd delivered early, and then . . .

"Dad." Sophie cut him off. "I can only talk for a few minutes. I fear things have gone wrong, and I need to catch you up." She briefly sketched in the disappearance of the rescue party and the contact she had made with Armita. "I'm here in Bangkok and about to find out if this message was really from Armita, or . . . if it is something else."

"Don't go alone," Frank said. "Wait. Let Security Solutions fly out there—hell, I'll beg Ellie to go. Ellie, my girl needs help!" Frank bellowed, addressing someone else in the room.

Sophie could clearly picture the elegant, blue-eyed brunette Secret Service agent who was assigned to her dad. She liked and respected Ellie Smith, but she was sure there was nothing the agent could do about something so far outside of her job parameters.

"Dad. No one can help me. The message I received said to come alone. And this is definitely not Ellie's area of responsibility." Sophie bit her lip. "I wish I could afford to wait for some kind of backup. But I believe Armita has broken away from Pim Wat to bring me my child; and if so, they are both in danger from her."

"Your mother! I still can't believe what an evil bitch she's turned out to be!"

"I know. I'm shocked too, and it hurts every day that we were so duped by her. I have to go, Dad, but I wanted you to know what's been happening. I will call you back as soon as I know anything. And if you really want to apply some pressure for me, call the CIA. Ask for Agent Devin McDonald. Lean on him to get our men back from the Yām Khûmkạn stronghold. I believe McDonald's the only one who might be able to do something. Bye, Dad. I love you." She ended the call.

She was trembling and sweaty. It had not reassured her to talk to Frank—his wild and anxious emotions had activated her own.

Sophie left a pile of *baht* for the maid and the bellboy who would deal with her backpack's storage, and slipped out of the room and down the servant's stairs. She exited the hotel into a back alley reeking of rotten food and piled with garbage. Making sure her veil was in place, Sophie hugged her voluminous garments close as she made her way around muddy puddles to the main thoroughfare.

She waved down one of the many taxi motor scooters with side cars that ferried the busy streets. Her native tongue came back easily as she haggled over the fare to take her ten miles outside of the city limits to the suburban area where her childhood home was situated.

Once again, Sophie wondered about contacting her favorite aunt, Malee, her mother's younger sister. Her namesake would not betray her . . . *Would she?*

But Malee might feel divided loyalty toward Pim Wat. Or her phone could be bugged. Sophie couldn't take a chance on either. No, she couldn't make contact except in person.

Hoisting her skirts higher than was strictly modest, Sophie wedged herself and her nylon bag into the sidecar of the scooter. She donned the greasy helmet the driver handed her, enduring the smell of clove cigarettes, and was grateful for the extra protection of the Muslim head covering as she buckled the chin strap over the fabric. She held on tight as the scooter took off with a lurch.

Sophie's motorcycle taxi driver was no worse than many on the street. He delivered her, relatively intact if a bit bruised and mud-spattered, at the corner of the road containing both her aunt's house and her former home. Sophie wiped muck off her face with the edge of her scarf and handed the helmet back to the driver, haggling once again over the tip.

Once the scooter was gone, Sophie turned to face the quiet street lined with ornamental orchid trees, their spreading branches bright with showy purple and white blooms. She walked down the mud brick sidewalk, scanning the spiked walls protecting gracious homes just off of the mighty Ping River. She could see the green gleam of the river and its community dock through the trees lining the street, and she felt her heart lift in spite of everything.

She hadn't been here for close to twenty years, but a part of her would always recognize this place as home.

Her aunt's and her parents' former houses were adjacent properties sharing a fence line. Sophie walked to her aunt's home. She stared longingly at Aunt Malee's front gate, a wooden affair decorated with much native carving and scrollwork, inset within an elaborate but sturdy frame. A beaded chain threaded through a hole beside the portal would ring a bell inside the compound to request admission.

Sophie longed to pull that chain—to hear the chimes within her aunt's home. She longed to see Malee's dear, pretty face, feel her aunt's loving arms around her in a hug, and smell her signature lemon and gardenia scent.

But she couldn't risk making contact yet.

She had to assess for threats first, and the best way to do that was to go in the side gate. *If only Auntie hadn't changed the lock and her hidey-hole for the key . . .*

Sophie checked the street. A battered Jeep rattled by; a row of duckling-like small children, holding onto a rope held by a servant, giggled and chattered on their way to some outing. Once the coast was clear, Sophie sidled her way along her aunt's fence to a hidden side entrance used by the servants. A heavy brass lock inside a niche secured the door.

Sophie felt around a pile of rocks topped by a decorative stone orb beside the portal for the key her aunt used to keep there. Her breath whooshed out—*the key was still there!* Thank God some people didn't have Sophie's concerns about security.

Sophie unlocked the gate, pushed it open gently, and peered around it.

The aperture opened into her aunt's gardens, a lush mix of flowers on one side, and practical rows of lettuces, tomatoes, bok choy, and staked runner beans on the other.

Sophie stared up at the house, searching for any signs of detection.

The dwelling was a smaller version of Sophie's former abode, built high on wooden pilings in case of the nearby Ping River's floods. The steeply peaked roofs and windows were of traditional design, and the exterior was brightly painted in charming contrasting colors.

The windows' wooden shutters were closed. Sophie saw no signs of life inside or on the grounds, but the lushness and care given to the gardens belied abandonment.

Sophie adjusted her garments, hoping that none of her aunt's servants were about—the last time she'd been here, her aunt had employed a couple of gardeners, housemaids, and a cook. If anyone confronted her, she planned to tell them the truth: she was Malee's niece, come to visit. But no interference came as Sophie worked her way to the other side of the garden, moving along the fence between the two properties.

Sophie squeezed through the runner beans and bee-laden sunflowers to the loose board she remembered from the last time she had sneaked over to play with her cousins. As she pushed at the fence, testing each board, she couldn't help smiling when the loose plank moved—it had appeared intact from the outside, and no one had nailed it back in.

Sophie was able to lift it away and peek through at her former home. Her heart thudded as she studied the large wooden house.

The shutters were closed and latched from the inside. Everything about the place had a neglected, abandoned look. She frowned as she took in the wild, overgrown grounds. Unlike her aunt's place, the vegetable garden was a barren mound of leaves and yard debris, and the flower garden a sad morass of dried stalks and bent over seed heads.

The place looked like it had been deserted for years.

The property had been bought by a company, Mutual Imports, and the purpose on the documents she'd uncovered had been described as a "corporate retreat center." Sophie wished she could go online now and dig a little deeper—the extreme neglect indicated the house had never been used for anything at all. She even spotted her father's antique Mercedes, a project car he'd worked on during his brief times at home, still parked under the deck and covered with a filthy canvas.

Sophie tightened her voluminous garments and sucked in her stomach, wriggling through the gap in the fence. Her larger breasts and still-soft belly caught on the splintery wood; she had to work hard to squeeze through the narrow opening, grateful that a spreading berry bush concealed her vigorous movements from the house.

After replacing the board, Sophie hurried through the tangled undergrowth and slipped beneath the house. As soon as she was in the shadows cast by the building, she heard the creak of a floorboard overhead.

Someone was inside.

CHAPTER TWENTY-FIVE

Sophie caught her breath at the sound of footsteps from above. She slid out of sight to take shelter under one of the large peeled logs that held up the two-story dwelling. The space beneath had been kept uncluttered in case of flooding, but was used for storage of unimportant items: stacks of fish traps, gardening tools, her father's old car, and even a small scooter, thick with dust.

Sophie's heart squeezed at the sight of a large woven basket filled with discarded children's toys. She remembered that red truck, that traditional doll with its face paint peeling and garments moth-eaten, the purple soccer ball faded to pink from sun exposure. Whoever this company was, they had not altered anything left behind in her childhood home.

She would use that knowledge to her advantage.

Sophie tiptoed forward to the storage shed built directly under the main living area of the house. Once inside the dark, musty-smelling space, Sophie unslung her nylon bag, setting it down on a heavy wooden project bench and startling a mouse that skittered away with a squeak.

She opened her laptop and booted it up. While it was loading, she unwound the stiff fiber optic cable camera she liked to use for surveillance. A tiny node at one end was her eyes, a second, her ears.

Once again, she heard the creak of a footstep overhead. Now she could catch the murmur of voices.

And then, a sound that woke her entire system with a zap of pure adrenaline: the distinctive cry of a newborn baby.

The hairs on Sophie's entire body lifted. Her breasts ached and her nipples tightened. She actually felt her uterus contract. Tears sprang to her eyes. *That was her baby's voice!*

She had to stay calm and logical. She had to get audio and visual on whatever was going on in that room. She couldn't rush in blind.

Sophie closed her eyes and took deep breaths until the urge to tear down anything between herself and her child had passed.

Sophie climbed carefully up onto the gardening bench. She took out the sound dampened, battery operated drill she had used on clandestine jobs for the FBI. She targeted a spot in the corner of the ceiling that she remembered being directly below a large armchair. If the new owners hadn't even removed her old toys, perhaps they had left the inside furnishings of the house untouched, as well.

Sophie pressed her nose against her shoulder, trying not to inhale the wood dust that blew by on a warm stream from the drill as it whirred silently into the native hardwood floor above her. The last thing Sophie needed to do right now was to sneeze and give herself away. She felt the give of the drill as it punched through, and she withdrew it and set it down.

Sophie threaded a stiff fiber optic cable up through the hole she had made. The cable was flexible enough to bend and manipulate. She would look through it, using the window provided by her laptop.

She descended quietly from the workbench and plugged the cable into an exterior feed on her laptop. She pulled up the visual and plugged in an earbud to hear the audio.

The camera had, indeed, come up under the old armchair. An expanse of smooth dark wood floor in front of her was distorted by the convex surface of the camera's eye. Sophie struggled to interpret what she was seeing, and rotated the cable slowly, looking for the people whose voices she had heard.

A rapidly moving bare brown foot passed by her vantage point, coinciding with a creak from above. Sophie twisted the cable to follow the pair of feet, and leaned it back to track upward.

She was looking at a petite woman dressed in a calf length, bright pink skirt and white leggings. A long black braid hung down the back of her blouse.

The audio came in suddenly, and too loud. "Here. Let me take her a moment," in rapid Thai.

The woman turned. Sophie clapped a hand over her mouth to stifle a gasp.

She was looking at her beloved aunt Malee, her namesake!

And cradled in her aunt's arms, wrapped in a soft cream-colored blanket, was her daughter. Though Sophie had not spent long with her precious Momi, she instantly recognized her baby's profile topped by lush black curls.

This could still be a trap. Pim Wat could have sent the baby here to stay with her aunt, to be cared for.

But where was Armita?

Sophie had her answer as her aunt walked forward, putting the baby to her shoulder, and murmuring a lullaby to the fretful infant as she patted her back.

Armita sat on a padded bench against the wall. Her former nanny was dressed in simple black as was her wont. The flickering glow of an oil lamp lit against the gloom of the closed shutters lit her face.

Armita looked tired. Dark circles ringed her eyes and a scratch marked her cheek. She seemed sad too—disheartened. *Perhaps she was about to give up on Sophie.*

Sophie calmed herself with difficulty.

She forced herself to manipulate the camera, turning it three hundred and sixty degrees to survey the entire room, checking for anyone else in the space.

The two women appeared to be alone.

Sophie's heart leapt with joy.

This wasn't a setup after all! Armita had risked her life to get Momi away from Pim Wat and bring her to a safe place, so they could be reunited.

Sophie pulled in the surveillance camera. Shut down the laptop. Repacked everything into her nylon bag, her hands trembling with excitement.

In a moment, she would be holding her child.

Sophie picked up the nylon bag and did one more visual sweep of the grounds, looking for a sentry or any other sign of hostiles—but there was none.

Just the two women she loved and trusted, and her baby crying fitfully and refusing to be comforted. *Crying for her mama.*

Sophie's whole body hummed with the need to get to her child. Some things were just elemental, biological, beyond understanding with the mind. Motherhood was one of those.

Hurrying on soft feet, Sophie climbed the stairs to the inner door that led to the kitchen, an open room off of the living area. She was not surprised when the door was locked, but she was undeterred. She took out her lock picks, and in moments, had the simple mechanism disabled. Sophie pressed down on the lever, opened the door—and found herself staring into the double barrels of a Remington twelve-gauge.

CHAPTER TWENTY-SIX

Day Twenty-Seven

P IM W AT STARED out the bubbled glass window of the helicopter as it lifted off the stronghold's landing and storage area.

She really hated helicopter travel—too loud for her sensitive hearing. Since there was no anticipated need for a comm link, she had put in silicone earplugs and wore sound-deadening earmuffs on top of them. Those measures still weren't enough to screen out the loud, whirling roar of the blades overhead as they got underway.

Pim Wat had woken up that morning, sated but dissatisfied from her night of passion with the Master.

He had forbidden her any further contact with the prisoners, reiterating that he had a plan and he would let her know if help was needed.

She was dismissed. Discounted. Even though the Master had reassured her of his love for her, she felt the sapping grief of her losses—and the restlessness of having no outlet for her frustration. She was a cat denied her mouse, and she knew it.

Perhaps shopping and distraction would help. She was overdue for a visit with her dear sister, Malee. Every time Pim Wat left after visiting that boring, poky house right next to the one she used to live in, Pim Wat felt better about her choices: she was an exotic phoenix who flew free with a lover who was a dragon among men. Malee was a mere chicken, with a tiny coop and a rooster who was seldom home.

Malee would give her a listening ear, a comforting hug as she always did. Maybe they'd get their nails done or go shopping in Bangkok. There were no secrets between sisters. Well, except for Pim Wat's entire life . . .

Pim Wat couldn't help smiling, enjoying the thought of Malee's ignorance. Malee believed Pim Wat to be an idle socialite, dabbling in watercolors and yoga retreats while spending her time on useless vacations and charity projects, interspersed with depression episodes that were a result of her delicate constitution. It would be so entertaining to tell Malee the truth someday, to list her kills and means of execution. She could just imagine the expression of shock and horror on her sister's bland face. Malee was a simple, loving, unimaginative woman.

Pim Wat's unseeing eyes tracked over the jungle mountains, rivers, and rice paddies below as she mulled over the conversation with the Master from the night before.

It was clear that she had been pulled off of the situation with her daughter. She knew better than to defy the Master; he might love her, but she had experienced his punishments before. He was an expert in the use of pain, but that had never been as effective on Pim Wat as the mere withdrawal of his presence, of his favor.

She suffered without him—it was that simple. "Curse it," she muttered, unable to even hear her voice through all the helicopter's racket. "I hate loving him."

Loving the Master made her weak like nothing else ever had. But she couldn't seem to turn off her emotions or harness them. Just the sound of his voice made her insides melt, made her turn herself inside out to please him.

Maybe someday she'd find a way to "wrap him around her

finger" as Frank used to say, but until then, she would just take these trips when she needed to—to demonstrate her independence, to remind herself of the reasons she lived the way she did.

Frank. What a farce that marriage had been. Pim Wat had been so depressed by childbirth and her life with that big, loud American with his endless career demands, that she'd taken to her bed to escape it—which turned out to be a handy cover as the years went by —and then, she met the Master. He recruited her, and gifted her with the role of a lifetime, her true calling as an assassin for the cause.

Too bad Sophie had turned out to be such a disappointment—but Pim Wat really couldn't blame her daughter's rebellion, after the marriage Pim Wat had arranged to Assan Ang had turned out to be such a disaster.

And then Sophie gave birth to a daughter.

Beautiful little thing, too, with a gentle disposition. Pim Wat had a good reason to steal the baby, and then when the child wasn't a match to the crown prince, she had seen a second chance to be a mother properly. She would have been, too, if that evil bitch Armita hadn't stolen her granddaughter . . .

"Thirty minutes to landing," the pilot said, and his voice vibrated obnoxiously through her earplugs. Pim Wat squinted irritably at him.

She would call her sister as soon as she landed. *Wouldn't Malee be surprised and pleased to see her!*

CHAPTER TWENTY-SEVEN

Day Twenty-Seven

"DON'T MOVE or I'll shoot." Armita's voice trembled, but the shotgun aimed at Sophie's midsection looked rock steady.

Sophie dropped her lockpicks and raised her hands. "Armita! It's Sophie!"

"Show me your face."

Sophie was the one with the trembling hand now, as she fumbled with the detachable face veil. The transparent black panel fell away, and Sophie pushed the headscarf back.

Armita's resolute face broke into a smile. She lowered the shotgun. "We were beginning to worry that something had happened to you. Your aunt and your child are in the other room, waiting for you."

"I can hear that." Momi's crying had ratcheted up a notch to a screech that brought all of Sophie's nerves rearing up. "I want to know everything that's happened, but first I must see my baby." She bent to embrace Armita's petite form, feeling the woman's wiry strength and slender bones. "There will never be enough thanks in the world for what you've done."

Armita cleared her throat. "Go quiet your child before she wakes the neighborhood."

Sophie hurried past her nanny to face her aunt in the living room. Malee's face, much like Pim Wat's but rounder and softer, was wreathed in smiles as she joggled the howling infant. "At last, you got here! We were beginning to wonder."

Sophie put her arms around Malee, sandwiching the baby between the two of them as she greeted her aunt with a heartfelt hug. "I am so happy to see you."

Momi's shrieking stilled as she was pressed between the two women in their loving embrace. Her scrunched-up eyes opened, and she gave a little squirm and wriggle, snuffling around, clearly hungry.

Sophie backed away and held out her arms. "May I?"

"Of course! She is yours." Malee pressed the wrapped bundle into Sophie's arms with alacrity.

The world narrowed to the tiny face pressed against her breast, to golden brown eyes fastened on hers.

Curly black halo of hair.

Stitchery of tiny brows, more a placeholder than an actual feature.

Soft, velvety, tawny-skinned cheeks.

A little button nose.

Pouting bud of mouth, working as if to get ready for another wail.

She was so adorable . . .

Momi arched her back, opened her mouth, and let out a powerful bellow that made all three women jump.

"She's hungry," Armita said. "I was heating her bottle. I had a wet nurse for her at the compound, but she has been taking the formula and bottle just fine since we left." Armita gestured to a pan resting on the gas stove. A small glass bottle of milk heated in water just beginning to steam around it.

Sophie's breasts ached. *Maybe there was still something left for her daughter*. But no. She already knew there wasn't. As Momi wound up for another howl, Sophie blinked back tears and held out her hand. Armita slipped the bottle of warm milk into it without a word, and Sophie placed it between her daughter's searching lips.

The three of them sighed in relief as the infant settled, sucking hard and seeming to hum to herself as she found comforting nourishment.

"I don't know if I will ever get tired of looking at her face," Sophie said.

"You never will. I never have."

Armita's hand squeezed her shoulder, and Sophie met her nanny's loving gaze with a smile. Sophie looked back down at her daughter. She slid a finger into Momi's grasping hand, marveling at the beauty of her tiny digits, the flexing of long fingers that were the exact shape of Sophie's own. "I cannot believe I'm holding her again."

"I hurt for your suffering, being without her," Armita said. "I could not go along once I discovered what they wanted her for."

Sophie frowned. "Why did Pim Wat take her?"

"The crown prince of Thailand is sick with leukemia."

Sophie gasped. "Oh no! He's just a child."

"Yes. And you, Sophie, are a match to give him a needed bone marrow transplant." Armita met Sophie's eyes. "You are his second cousin. Everyone around him, and throughout the court, has been tested, and your DNA was on file after your kidnapping as a child. You are the only match that has been discovered. Pim Wat hoped that Momi might be one, so she took her. Taking the marrow sample from Momi's hip was . . ." Armita shut her eyes. "It is a painful test with a big needle for such a small body. She is not a match."

Sophie's breath caught and she squeezed the baby tightly, hardly able to endure imagining the procedure. "And after Mother found out that my child could not donate?"

"Pim Wat decided to keep her. To try again to have a daughter."

"As if she were a stray puppy she had decided to adopt," Sophie ground out.

"I'm afraid so. I could not watch her do what she did to you, all over again."

"And after Armita contacted me about what my sister was doing, I told her we had to get the baby back to you," Malee said. "We decided Armita would hide here until you could come get the two of them."

Sophie met Armita's gaze. "How did you get away from the stronghold?"

Armita stroked the baby's soft curls as she spoke. "I have a few friends among the Yām Khûmkạn; but the truth is, the Master was not excited about having a child in the stronghold. He did not like having Pim Wat's attention distracted from him and his missions for her. He allowed us to get away. Turned a blind eye."

"The Master?"

Armita sighed. "How he came into Pim Wat's life is a long story. But the summary is that the Master is the leader of the Yām Khûmkạn, and your mother's lover. A very powerful man. I would venture to say, more powerful even than the king, though he is sworn to protect the monarchy."

"How is it that I have never heard of this man? I have researched the Yām Khûmkạn extensively." Sophie felt drunk on her daughter's sweet, milky smell. She tucked her nose in beside Momi's neck for a deep inhale. She loved the feel of Momi's weight, the tiny grunts and rumbles the baby emitted—her daughter was altogether addicting.

"The Master stays in the shadows. He allows no photographs, has no footprint, carries no name. He is . . ."

"Evil," Malee said over her shoulder. She had begun washing up in the kitchen, and she splashed angrily at the sink.

"I don't think evil is correct," Armita said in her measured way. "There is compassion in the Master. He is kinder than Pim Wat has ever been. But he does not hesitate to kill and to use any means necessary to control those around him. He rules absolutely." Armita's words were thoughtful, as if she had considered them a long time. "He's not evil. But he *is* ruthless."

"I suspect that this Master has my men." Sophie filled the two women in on the missing rescue party. "Now that my child and I are reunited, my attention must turn to getting Jake, Connor, and the other men back. Did you see any sign of them at the compound? Hear anything about their capture?"

"I did not. But that isn't surprising. It is a large place, and I stayed in Pim Wat's apartments. Only a few women are allowed on the base, and only in just a few areas. There is little to no technology in the compound." Armita shook her head. "Getting the men back will not be easy. The stronghold is well-defended."

"I have been trying to get the attention of the CIA," Sophie said. "I have offered to become their informant if they will help me. I am in communication with our security agency in Hawaii, as well, but they have had no luck getting any help from the authorities."

"As for me, I am worried about Pim Wat coming after Armita," Malee said. "I bought this house—your former home—under a shell company with your uncle. I did it to keep it in the family—I thought you might want to return someday." Malee wiped down the counter with a cloth as Sophie had seen her do a hundred times. "Seemed like a good investment, to have it available next door. And it has been."

"I thank you, Auntie," Sophie said. "Does Pim Wat know that you own this place?"

"My sister thinks I am a sheep." Malee smiled darkly. "I am not. I have many secrets from Pim Wat, this house not least of them."

Malee and Armita had provided the nurture that Sophie had needed as a child. Affection surged up in her for the two brave women. "I want to take you back to the island where I was hiding—but I'm concerned that one of the men may have given up that location to Pim Wat and the Master. We are better off flying directly to Hawaii when we can get transport—we will be safer back in the

United States." Momi had fallen asleep at last, and Sophie gazed at the baby's sweet face.

"You two go. I will stay here. My sister will never know I was involved," Malee said.

Sophie nodded, settling the sleeping baby close. She had no desire to set the infant down. *Ever.*

"Momi still needs to be burped," Armita instructed. "Otherwise gas will wake her up later."

Sophie lifted her daughter up against her shoulder and patted her back carefully, unwilling to wake the child after all of the stress of her screaming.

Malee's phone buzzed, startling the baby, and Sophie glanced over to see Malee gasp as she checked the caller. "It's Pim Wat!"

Sophie stood up carefully, preparing to flee to another room if the baby cried, as Malee took the call.

"Sister!" Malee said cheerfully in Thai, pulling a face that would have been funny if the stakes hadn't been so high. Sophie appreciated Malee's effort to minimize Pim Wat's threat—but she wasn't fooled. Pim Wat might well take pleasure in killing Armita, to begin with. *No telling what she'd do to Sophie, Momi, and even her own sister if she discovered she had been double—crossed . . .*

Malee had put Pim Wat on speaker, so that the three of them could hear her husky voice clearly. "Malee. I'm on my way to see you. I need a break."

"A break from what? Your busy round of art openings and fashion shows?" Malee continued to clown, rolling her eyes, communicating clearly that she was keeping up the fiction that she didn't know anything about her deadly sister's real lifestyle.

"I'll tell you all about it when I get to your place. I just landed in Bangkok and I should be at your house in about half an hour."

Three pairs of eyes widened in alarm. Sophie squeezed the baby inadvertently, and Momi let out a sleepy belch at last.

"I can't wait to see you, sister! We'll do pedicures," Malee said with forced cheer, and ended the call.

CHAPTER TWENTY-EIGHT

Day Twenty-Seven

A GONG SOUNDED SOMEWHERE in the depths of the stronghold, waking Connor. The recruits in the barracks room he'd been billeted with got up in silence, rolling their bedclothes into neat bundles and dressing in all black *gi*.

Connor had slept poorly. He'd been tied, loosely enough to sleep, but too tightly to make any attempt to escape; the other men ignored him. He was a white-skinned pariah lying on his little pallet in the corner.

Connor waited, his bladder painfully full, as they departed in silence. That must be part of their daily ritual. Finally, the ninja who'd helped Connor before returned to untie him.

Connor studied the man's shorn head—a Thai number was inked onto the back of his naked scalp. "What is your name?" Connor asked, in halting Thai.

The man looked up swiftly. "You speak our language."

"A little." Connor held up a finger and thumb with a narrow space between them. He tried a disarming grin.

"My name is Nine of House. You can call me Nine." Nine was

dead serious and focused on undoing knots in the natural hemp rope that had tightened during the night.

"Nine. That is an unusual name."

"We take a new name when we join the Yām Khûmkạn. We have a designation, and the area we serve. I serve the House—the living quarters of the Master and our leaders."

"My name is . . . Connor." He surprised himself by speaking the truth. Only a handful of people in the world knew his real first name, but his stratagems, so necessary elsewhere, seemed irrelevant here.

"Come, then, Connor." Nine tugged Connor up by his arm once the ropes were off. "Hurry. You must be clean and ready to be in the presence of the Master."

Connor didn't like the sound of that, but resistance would get him nowhere—he was outmanned and outmaneuvered. He followed Nine down empty stone hallways lit by slits high near the ceiling. Bars of stark white sunlight beamed through them into the gloomy passageway. Some of these sun spots were cleverly directed, using polished brass mirrors set on the floor and tilted to light different areas, a low-tech way to keep the interior lit. The Egyptians had used such techniques in the Pyramids.

Nine led Connor down several sets of cut stone stairs to a large bathhouse. Water from hot springs formed sulfurous steam in a man-made pool. Nine showed him a bowl of soft vegetable-based soap, and gestured. "Get clean. Dress in a robe over there." He pointed to a wall lined with pegs where black *gi* hung in rows.

The mineral-rich water stung a bit, but also soothed Connor's cuts and bruises. He cleaned himself and dressed. Following Nine back up the stairs to meet the Master, Connor felt his abs tightening with apprehension.

What was going to happen today? More torture? As he'd tossed and turned on his pallet, thinking over what the Master had said the day before, he'd come up with a plan—but just thinking about implementing it dried his mouth.

Nine led Connor out of the main building, through a courtyard filled with practicing ninjas, and down a short flight of stairs to a walled terrace garden.

A gravity-fed fountain trickled into a koi pond lined with water lilies. Smooth grass encircled the pond; beds of herbs and flowers lined the stone walls. A table and chairs were set under a flowering tree.

And across from the pond, the Master sat balanced on the top of a six-foot high plinth made of glowing tiger's eye.

The column of beautifully carved gemstone caught the morning light, glowing as if lit from within. There was no visible way the man could have gotten up there, and the pillar upon which he sat was no more than a foot in diameter.

The Master was absolutely still, cross-legged in a meditation pose, his fingers held in a mudra, his eyes closed. He looked like a statue in his white *gi* atop the post.

Nine inclined his head toward the seating area under the tree, and left. Connor walked over and sat down at the table. Tea steeped in a porcelain pot; covered bowls on a tray emitted delicious smells. Connor's belly rumbled.

"If you train with me, you will learn to control all aspects of your bodily functions." The Master's voice carried clearly, though not amplified in any way Connor could discern. "Including the sounds of your belly."

The Master planted his hands between his crossed legs on the top of the plinth. Slowly he extended his legs, lifting his lower body off the plinth. He rolled his head forward and down, and then, in an act of extreme strength and controlled grace, lifted himself up into a handstand. Completely vertical above the plinth, the Master stayed perfectly still.

He held the pose beyond what seemed humanly possible—and then, in a whirl of movement almost too fast to follow, flipped and landed on the grass.

The Master walked over to Connor and looked down at him. "Pour the tea."

The man wasn't even winded.

Connor poured the tea. The Master uncovered bowls of fruit, scrambled eggs, nuts and fried rice that made Connor's mouth water.

Connor waited until the Master had served them both and taken a bite, before he dug into his breakfast with a pair of chopsticks. The food was delicious. Once again, he had to try not to eat too quickly—but he'd been hungry for a long time, and last night's dinner had burned off already.

When they'd mostly finished their meal, the Master spoke. "Have you thought over what I asked you yesterday?"

"What was the question?" Connor sipped his tea and kept his gaze averted, buying time—the Master always seemed to see more than Connor wanted him to.

"I asked you if you wanted to learn."

"I can't just stay here. I run a multimillion dollar company. I have responsibilities . . ." Connor ran out of steam. *If the Master knew he was the Ghost, he likely knew the rest too.*

He had no family. No lover. He had Sophie, but only as a friend. He had his many interests, not least of them righting the scales of justice. He had a company, an island, a dog, a neglected violin, and a lot of money.

"No one will miss you. You have nothing to lose," the Master said gently.

Connor suppressed a wince. "I have a life, little as you seem to think of it. What do you want from me?"

"I want you to bring Sophie here to donate bone marrow to the crown prince."

"I have been thinking about that. But I won't ask her to come here, to this fortress. Instead, I could ask her to go to the hospital in Bangkok. It's likely she will, as I said before. She loves children, and the prince is family." Connor set down his teacup. "But I have some things that I want in exchange."

"Such as?" The Master raised a brow.

"I want you to let Jake go. Sophie needs him. And I want you to make Pim Wat leave Sophie and her daughter alone after she gives the prince her bone marrow. If you do those two things, I will stay here and learn with you." Nervous sweat broke out on Connor's body in an uncomfortable, prickly flush, but it gradually faded as the Master stared at him.

Those damn purple eyes . . .

"You love Sophie. That's why you'll trade yourself for her lover."

There was no point in lying. "Yes."

"Then, I find your offer acceptable. I will let Jake go." The Master turned away and stared out over the pond contemplatively. "Finish your breakfast—you will need your strength. Training will begin this afternoon."

CHAPTER TWENTY-NINE

Day Twenty-Seven

P IM W AT ENTERED her sister's house when Malee opened the door. "This is a surprise! Glad you called, I was in the middle of something," Malee said.

"I had to get away for a few days." Pim Wat embraced Malee, and they air kissed. Malee stood back, studying Pim Wat's face. "You look terrible, sister! What's been going on?"

Pim Wat felt quick tears flood her eyes. That was the thing about Malee; she was one of the only people Pim Wat trusted with her emotional state, even if she lied about the reasons for it. "Armita has run off."

"Oh no! Why would Armita do that? She's been with you for so long!" Malee's eyes went wide with surprise.

Of course, Pim Wat couldn't tell Malee that she had stolen Sophie's baby. Malee would never approve of Pim Wat's actions in that regard. She had been horrified when Pim Wat hinted that she wanted to adopt Sophie's child, complaining that her daughter was an unfit mother, what with her depression and dangerous activities.

Malee hadn't liked those comments. Malee had a soft spot for

Sophie, one that Pim Wat had encouraged when Sophie was young, knowing that her daughter needed the softness and nurturing Malee provided.

"I don't know why Armita left. She didn't even leave me a note, just cleaned out her clothes and disappeared." Pim Wat felt her lip trembling. "Faithless wench. No better than any other hireling."

"How terrible," Malee said, but even though her words portrayed that feeling, she didn't mean it. Pim Wat wasn't the most sensitive person in the world; she knew this, and accepted it about herself. *But Malee was someone Pim Wat knew well.*

Her sister was faking both her surprise, and her concern.

Pim Wat grabbed Malee, digging her daggerlike fingernails into her sister's arms. "Did Armita contact you?"

Malee flung Pim Wat's clutching hands off with a snort. "Ha. As if I'd give your maid the time of day!"

"You're lying." Pim Wat grabbed her sister again, staring into large brown eyes much like her own. "Where is Armita?"

"I don't know what you're talking about." Malee drew a shaky breath and dropped her eyes. "I am upset this morning. That is all. I think someone has . . . broken into the house."

Pim Wat let go of her sister and stepped back, cocking her head to the side as she studied Malee's face. "What makes you think so?"

Malee turned away, wringing her hands nervously. "Some things are moved. I was just getting ready to try to search the house and find out what had been taken when you called to let me know you were coming. I'm just unsettled."

"So, you don't actually know if anyone was inside?"

Malee hung her head, bit her lip. "I left the downstairs door open. Maybe they came in from outside. I think some of the silver might be missing."

"Well, you know better than to bother notifying the police," Pim Wat said acerbically. Local law enforcement was notoriously corrupt. "Let's figure this out. I'd rather do that than get our nails done." Pim Wat put her hands on her hips and surveyed the traditionally decorated room, then clapped her hands abruptly. "I have an idea. I remember something!" Pim Wat grabbed Malee's arm again, and gave it a tug. "Let's go outside. I might know how they got into your property. Closing up any loopholes is the smartest thing to do before you get into finding out what's gone."

Malee dug in her heels. "No hurry. Let's have some tea first." Was her face pale? Pim Wat was determined to figure out this mystery. *Her sister was hiding something.*

Pim Wat tugged a protesting Malee down the stairs and out into the garden area. Searching back and forth, she spotted it: that loose board in the fence that Sophie used to sneak through when she came over to play with her cousins.

"What are you doing? I am tired of this. I'll just wait until my husband gets home. We will both deal with it then . . ." Pim Wat paid no heed to her sister's protestations as she dragged Malee through the gardens and over to the fence.

Pim Wat felt along the weathered boards until she identified the loose one. She lifted it out of place easily and set it aside.

"Here it is! Sophie used to come over from our side through this. You've really got to get this fixed." Pim Wat peered into the yard next door. "Oh, it's sad to see our old home fallen into such neglect. That company that bought the property never did a thing with it!"

Pim Wat stared up at the shuttered dark bulk of her former home, overwhelmed with memories as she always was when she was reminded of her unhappy time living there.

She frowned to see a sliver of light gleaming through one of the shutters. She let go of Malee's arm to point. "Look! There's someone inside!" She turned back to her sister.

One look at Malee's face, and she *knew.*

The blood drained from Pim Wat's head. She was dizzy and sick with hurt—and then anger surged back. "You helped her! Armita's hiding in there!"

Familiar, comforting rage, with all of its strength and none of her doubts, swept through her. Cementing her conviction, Pim Wat heard the thin wail of a crying baby. "You helped Armita escape. You hid them both."

"No!" Malee backed away, slapping at Pim Wat's grasping claws, her eyes wide and frightened. "I don't know what you're talking about. You sound like a crazy person."

Pim Wat stalked forward and got her hands around Malee's throat. "How dare you betray me? My own sister!"

Correct placement of fingers was important in strangulation. Each digit mattered when killing quickly and humanely, pressing over significant nerve clusters as well as veins and arteries, and of course, the airway. She needed to get this over with quickly.

After all, this was her dear, close sister, not just some random contract.

Pim Wat ignored the pleading and terror in Malee's bulging eyes as her sister made awful sounds, her nails scratching at Pim Wat's wrists. If Pim Wat felt a stab of grief and regret, along with the rage, that was just as well. Her sister represented emotional weakness, and she would eliminate that, once and for all.

She pressed harder, just so.

Malee went limp, and her begging eyes shut at last.

CHAPTER THIRTY

Day Twenty-Seven

JAKE WOKE from another day of sleep in what he had begun to think of as his cell. He had been there for two days. Nothing had gone on but eating, first aid, and sleeping, interspersed with awful episodes of thinking.

He stared up at the stone ceiling. Finally, his head was clear and his body was only mildly aching. This was the first time that he'd felt really returned from the dead.

But he had no interest in getting up. The needs of his body were merely irritating intrusions; he just wanted more pain meds so he could keep sleeping. The grief and betrayal of his discovery about Connor and Sophie had left him in a deep black mood.

The old Jake would have spent hours doing isometric exercises in the cell, plotting an escape.

The new Jake couldn't find a reason to care about any of it.

Was this what Sophie went through when she had her depressive episodes? If so, he finally understood a little more what a little slice of hell must be like—because even when Jake tried to flog himself into getting up and exercising, he could hardly make himself stagger to the chamber pot in the corner.

He should at least push open the door and see what was out in the hall—but he just didn't care. In fact, he was pretty sure it would've been better if he'd died.

Jake cringed at the memory of the heartfelt letter he had left Sophie in case of his demise. He'd asked her to marry him during the pregnancy and she'd said, "It's not the right time." He hadn't pressed, figuring she wanted to get through the birth before making their relationship official, but when leaving on the mission, he'd wanted to make sure she knew how he felt, what he wanted for their future.

He'd put the letter on the side table next to her bed, along with his grandmother's ring. The beautiful cushion-cut, one carat stone set in a platinum band had a low profile that he thought Sophie could get used to wearing—and if something happened to him, he'd wanted her to have it, regardless.

But now that he knew Connor's identity, he couldn't help wondering if there was something more behind her refusal.

The thoughts tormented him like stinging flies. He groaned aloud, unable to find any other way to express the pain clouding his mind and echoing through his body.

The door creaked open and he looked over to see the healer standing there. "Get up. You are being set free."

Jake frowned. "Has someone come for me? Have they made a deal?"

The healer shook his head. "I am to give you something to take with you for your wounds." He gestured to the various bruises and abrasions still decorating Jake's body. He handed Jake a little pot of salve. "And here is clothing." He thrust a clean *gi* into Jake's lap.

Even with this incredible news, Jake had to force himself to stand up, to pull on the rough cotton clothing, to slide the small clay pot of ointment into his pocket. "Is someone waiting for me?"

Again, the healer shook his head, refusing to answer.

Jake followed the man out of the infirmary area. He was silently stared at, his height and pale skin making him distinctive, as they made their way through a maze of stone passageways—but no one stopped them.

Connor had either caved and given up Sophie and his island hideout, or someone had made a deal with the purple-eyed leader.

Jake followed the healer out into a courtyard.

Rows of ninjas practicing their martial arts routines filled the area. The purple-eyed man, dressed in his signature white, paced back and forth at the head of the lines of shaved-headed recruits, his eye upon the trainees for any imperfection.

Jake's gaze was drawn to a man in the back row, taller than the rest.

A white man. With blue eyes and a shaved head.

Connor.

Fury rose up in Jake—Connor had made some kind of deal. He'd sold off information to send Jake on his way. And worst of all, he had *betrayed* him. Kept him in the dark. Lied to him! God only knew what the man's real relationship was with Sophie.

All lassitude fell away as adrenaline flushed through Jake. He broke from behind the healer and charged across the open area of the square, headed straight for his target like a heat-seeking missile. "I know who you are! Whatever deal you made, you made with the devil, you cheating bastard!"

Ninjas engulfed Jake in a black-clad wave, swarming over him and burying him in sheer numbers. Of course, he didn't make it through all of them to pound Connor out, but he at least made it far enough to have the satisfaction of seeing fear and devastation in the man's ocean-colored eyes.

"I know who you are!" Jake bellowed as he was borne bodily away, a cluster of ninjas clinging to every limb as they hustled him out of the courtyard. "And I'm gonna kick your ass, count on it, if I have to wait a lifetime!"

The dustup invigorated Jake at last, and he welcomed the

ongoing scuffle as his own personal mob of ninjas, directed by the healer, escorted him unceremoniously through the compound and thrust him bodily out through a great wooden gate.

Jake stumbled and fell to his knees onto the dirt road outside the compound. The gate slammed shut behind him.

He stood up. Dusted off his clothing. Turned back and looked at the compound.

A row of unfamiliar faces stared down at him from the parapets. He didn't see Connor, Pim Wat, the healer, or even the purple-eyed man. Just a row of mocking faces, yelling insults at him in Thai.

"Eat shit and die, assholes." He flipped them the bird and turned away, heading down the muddy track into the jungle at a ground-eating lope.

CHAPTER THIRTY-ONE

Day Twenty-Seven

WATCHING FROM THE WINDOW ABOVE, Sophie saw Pim Wat grab Malee by the throat. *Pim Wat must have guessed that they were hiding in the house, and now she was killing her sister.* "The jig is up," as Marcella would say.

Sophie thrust Momi, who'd given their position away with her fussing, into her portable bassinet. She drew her weapon and flew down the stairs. She was sure the sound of her running footsteps on the wooden stairs would alert Pim Wat to her presence, but her mother was staring too intently into her sister's darkening face and bulging eyes to pay any attention as Sophie barreled through the unkempt yard. "Mother! Stop!"

Pim Wat looked up at last. Her eyes dilated in shock—and Sophie used all the momentum of her running force to slam the butt of her pistol into her mother's head.

Pim Wat dropped like a bag of dirty laundry to the ground, unconscious. Malee fell too, as Pim Wat's hands left her throat.

Sophie shoved her mother aside with her foot and dropped to her knees beside Malee, feeling for a pulse at her aunt's throat.

Yes! Malee's heart was still beating!

In her anxiety, Sophie couldn't remember what exactly she was supposed to do next, but found herself leaning over Malee's body, blowing into her mouth.

A couple of moments later, Malee came around, choking and coughing as her breathing reflex activated. Sophie sat Malee up, holding her cradled in her arms.

"Ahhhh!"

That powerful cry brought Sophie's head up.

The sound had burst from Armita's lips as the nanny ran toward them from the house. She carried a butcher knife in each hand, and she was barreling toward Pim Wat's supine body.

Sophie stood up and stepped into the maid's path, extending a hand with her palm up to stop Armita's headlong rush. "No! I can't let you kill her. I want to trade her for help from the CIA."

Armita stood over Pim Wat's crumpled body. "Please. She doesn't deserve to live. I understand if you can't do it. Please just let me kill her."

Sophie put her hands on Armita's shoulders and gave a gentle shake. "I can't imagine what your life, living under her thumb, has been like all of these years. She is truly a terrible person. I'm not stopping you from doing this because she deserves to live, or because she's my mother. I'm stopping you because she's more valuable to us alive. And, if it's a consolation, they will make her suffer in Guantánamo when they interview her for information on the Yām Khûmkạn."

Armita eventually allowed Sophie to remove the knives from her hands. Zombie-like, she turned and went back toward the house. Sophie frowned, and was relieved to see Armita headed toward the storage shed. The nanny returned with a length of electrical cord. She knelt and tied the unconscious Pim Wat cruelly, fastening her wrists to her ankles behind her back so that she was arched and helpless—and then Armita stood up and kicked her, hard.

"Thank you," was all Sophie said.

CHAPTER THIRTY-TWO

Day Twenty-Seven

JAKE JOGGED down the potholed jungle road. He had a long way to go to get to civilization, but at least he didn't have to do it bush-whacking through virgin jungle in stealth mode, the way he'd come. Thinking of that made him remember all the good men who'd died, coming with him and Connor for this stupid mistake of a mission.

Jake couldn't forget the sight of Connor's eyes, fearful and devastated. What was Connor afraid of? He wasn't scared of Jake physically—the dude was plenty brave. He was afraid of something else that Jake's words had told him—that Jake would rat him out as the Ghost vigilante to the authorities? Because that sure as hell would be happening.

And that other expression—sadness? Grief? What was that about? Was Connor actually sorry to lose Jake's friendship and trust? Or was it something else?

Connor's head was shaved. He was wearing the *gi* of the recruits. What was going on? Was the dude in trouble?

"Screw him," Jake growled. "Two-faced liar."

Jake ran on, his bare feet taking a beating on the uneven terrain—but walking just wasn't fast enough to get away from that place.

A dense tree tunnel engulfed the road. Arched branches of teak trees screened out the sunlight overhead, drawing a curtain of deep green darkness over the muddy road. Shrill cacklings and cries of animals, not small ones either, rang through the underbrush. The scream of a monkey overhead competed with the piercing cry of some bird giving an alarm. The smell of wet and rotting things, as well as green and growing things, filled Jake's nostrils.

The bodies of the men Pim Wat had executed, buried in that unmarked mass grave, would be halfway decomposed by now.

Jake fought down a wave of nausea. Death was a part of life, and especially a part of the life he had chosen. Any of them could go at any time; in fact, no one was getting out of here alive, even those who played it safe. *It had never been his style to play it safe.*

If it had been, he'd never have fallen for a woman like Sophie.

He had some hard questions for Sophie, and they'd make or break the future. For the first time since he realized that he was in love with her, Jake felt capable of walking away.

He'd died, and there was no heaven.

Jake emerged out of the tree tunnel.

The roar of an approaching helicopter brought his gaze up to the sky. Hours had passed and he was miles away from the Yām Khûmkạn stronghold. *Why would they be coming after him now?*

But the chopper dropping through the canopy into view to settle on the road ahead of him was a fully loaded American Apache, and he'd bet his left nut the Yām Khûmkạn didn't have one of those.

"Holy crap!" *He was being rescued.*

Jake forced his tired body into a last push forward.

He reached the chopper as a portly white man dressed in jungle camo got out of the chopper. "Jake Dunn?"

"Yep. Boy, am I glad to see you."

"Devin McDonald, CIA." The jowly agent shook Jake's hand and clapped him on the shoulder. "Hop aboard. The Yām Khûmkạn has plenty of anti-aircraft missiles at the compound, I happen to know, and they're allowing this pickup—but we shouldn't be around if they change their minds."

JAKE HAD WONDERED what kind of headquarters the CIA would have in Thailand, and he might have known it would be a five-star luxury hotel. Freshly shaved, showered, and shoveling in a gigantic room service porterhouse steak, Jake thought through the statement he would be making to the CIA.

As if reading his mind, McDonald, seated across from him in the room's dining area, wiped his mouth on a napkin and sat back with a belch. He lifted a glass of Châteauneuf-du-Pape in a brief salute. "To expense accounts."

Jake lifted his glass as well. "To a well-timed pickup. How did you guys know where I was going to be?"

"Sophie Smithson has been rather persistent in asking for help." The man set down his glass. "It took the agency a while to decide how we could assist. A full-frontal attack on the Yām Khûmkạn compound was out of the question for obvious reasons. But we set up surveillance on approaches to the compound, hoping that any of you who'd been on the mission would make an appearance. Where is everyone, anyway? I was given to understand you had ten men altogether."

Sophie. Sophie had badgered the CIA until they got off their butts . . . "You never had any intention of rescuing us?"

McDonald's cold blue eyes hardly blinked. "This situation went all the way to the Oval Office, if you can believe it, and we got no authorization for anything but a covert support transport." He took another sip of his wine. "I don't need to explain the diplomatic ramifications of acknowledging a mission like yours, let alone sanctioning a group of US mercenaries mounting an attack on the Yām Khûmkạn facility."

"We were never going to attack that damned place." Jake stretched his arms overhead, and rubbed his full belly with a sigh. "We were just going to investigate how to sneak in and get my daughter back."

He remembered, as suddenly as the words formed, that Momi wasn't his daughter. Never had been. He'd just decided to pretend she was, and love her like it was a done deal.

Well, nothing was a done deal in this life, least of all love.

"I heard about Sophie Smithson's kidnapped infant daughter from my contact in the Secret Service, Ellie Smith, even before Sophie reached out to me. Before Sophie became pregnant, we were negotiating with her to become a confidential informant on the Yām Khûmkan's activities. She and Sheldon Hamilton were our contacts and we were working on a strategy to surveille the compound and the major players of the Yām Khûmkan. After she got pregnant, she and Hamilton pulled the plug." McDonald leaned forward on his meaty arms and met Jake's eyes. "What's happened to Sheldon Hamilton? And where are the rest of your men?"

"Now that's a story that will take some telling. But first—do you know why I was released? Did Sophie, or anyone else—negotiate a deal with the Yām Khûmkan?"

"Nope. The agency was just keeping an eye on things, waiting for more intel, hoping someone would be set free as a goodwill gesture. Is that what your liberation was—a goodwill gesture?"

"I have no idea." Jake sat back and rubbed the back of his neck; a headache had begun as a persistent throb at the base of his skull. "I doubt good will had anything to do with it. Hamilton and I are the only ones left alive."

McDonald turned on a recorder, and Jake laid out the ambush they had experienced as they attempted to surveille the compound. "Pim Wat, Sophie's mother, killed everyone but me and Hamilton."

"We have a file on Pim Wat." McDonald's eyes gleamed. "She is more than the socialite she appears to be."

"No shit. And so is Hamilton." Jake owed Connor nothing. He

owed Sophie nothing. They had betrayed him, and now it was payback time. Jake laid out all he had put together regarding Hamilton's second identity. "Hamilton killed off the Todd Remarkian identity when the FBI was getting too close to blowing his cover."

McDonald splashed the last of the wine into their glasses. "Whoa. I will need time to verify all of this."

"Contact Marcella Scott of the FBI. She has been investigating the Ghost. And to make things even weirder, the last time I saw Hamilton, he was dressed as a ninja-trainee and was practicing martial arts with the other recruits of the Yām Khûmkạn. I think he might have made some kind of deal with the man with the purple eyes—unless Sophie did, first." Jake's belly cramped at the thought. How was he going to live with her betrayal? *How?*

"Sophie has been off the grid for days, so I don't think she was the one to negotiate your release." McDonald rubbed his bristly chin. "I don't know about you, but I have phone calls to make. I imagine you've got friends and family you want to reach out to, beginning with Sophie, to let them know you're safe. We can pick up this interview in the morning."

"Sure," Jake said hollowly. No way was he ready to talk to Sophie. "Got a scrambler phone I can borrow?"

CHAPTER THIRTY-THREE

Day Twenty-Eight

SOPHIE CUDDLED her daughter as she moved the hammock swing in an idle arc with her foot. The deck of her aunt's house, decorated with sturdy rattan outdoor furniture and pots of beautiful flowering shrubs, was a pleasant place in which to revel in sunshine, and Sophie enjoyed feeding Momi and a moment of solitude after a busy twenty-four hours.

She, Malee, and Armita had moved Pim Wat to the storage shed under Sophie's old house for an uncomfortable night in darkness and solitude as the three of them, with baby in tow and no further need for concealment, trooped back to Malee's house.

They'd talked in detail about what to do with Sophie's lethal and recalcitrant mother, who was reduced to an entirely manageable bundle of indignant squawks and evil glares now that she was bound and gagged.

But Sophie was worried. She couldn't keep her mother tied up forever and, at some point, the Master would miss her and come looking.

Sophie had already left a message for McDonald at the CIA. She needed to get Pim Wat off her hands and into their custody, but her mother was also a powerful bargaining chip for her men's lives.

Softhearted Malee had already wanted to let Pim Wat out of her dank prison, so now her mother was seated on a deck chair in the garden below as Malee moved among her sunflowers, deadheading and trimming, carrying on a monologue at her sister that Sophie enjoyed listening to. Malee was letting her sister know, in no uncertain terms, that many of the assumptions Pim Wat had made about her were incorrect; that, in fact, Pim Wat wasn't the only one to have engaged in both espionage and illicit business. Aunt Malee dabbled in opium smuggling to support her habit of buying real estate, such as Sophie's former home, and she was having a good brag about her various endeavors.

Watching Pim Wat have to listen, wriggling and snorting in her bindings, was disturbingly entertaining.

But the situation as it was could not go on. She had to try to reach McDonald again; it was time to make the call.

Sophie adjusted Momi in her baby sling, reassembled her satellite phone, and pressed the pre-programmed number for CIA Agent Devin McDonald.

McDonald came on immediately. "I was hoping to hear from you —in fact, I was about to call you myself."

"I take it there has been some movement from Washington regarding rescuing my men?" Sophie's heart rate picked up at the thought of being reunited with Jake and Connor.

"I was authorized to surveille and assist in any escape attempts, and one of your men was set free yesterday. I'm surprised he hasn't called you. I thought you two were involved."

"What? Who?" Sophie sat up abruptly, startling the baby into a yelp and flail of her tiny arms. "Who did you rescue?"

"Jake Dunn. As I said, I'm surprised he hasn't called you. I turned him loose yesterday with a sat phone to make calls."

"Maybe he just couldn't get through." Sophie frowned. "I've been frantic with worry. And what about Hamilton?"

"Yes, Hamilton." The CIA man cleared his throat. "Hamilton wasn't so lucky. He's still in the compound. But he's still better off than the other poor sons of bitches that were on your team. Dead, all of them, killed by your mother. I'm sorry . . ."

Sophie stared down into the garden at a bound and gagged Pim Wat, lying on the padded chaise lounge, still making indignant noises at her sister as Malee lectured her—a weirdly charming scene of sisterly togetherness. "Mother killed them all?"

"Yes. Gutted and beheaded them with a samurai sword." McDonald blew out a breath. Sophie could almost see the florid-faced man pinching the bridge of his nose. "I'm surprised to have to be the one to tell you this. I really thought Jake was going to call you yesterday."

"Where is Jake now?"

"Not sure. He's not a prisoner. We're staying in the Grand Palace Bangkok Hotel. He has his own room."

Jake was less than fifteen minutes away!

"Do you know why Jake was set free?" Sophie's belly roiled—*why hadn't he called her?* Armita came in, and, seeing Sophie's expression, lifted the baby out of the sling and walked away with the infant, giving Sophie space to deal with the situation.

"Jake claims not to know why they cut him loose. He thought maybe you got in touch with the leader, the man they call the Master, and made a deal."

"No, I have not. I've been too busy rescuing my daughter to do anything but call you and ask for help," Sophie said. "The good news is, I have my daughter back. And now I have a trade to propose to you. I've got someone to trade to you, in return for helping me get Hamilton out."

"What do you mean?" McDonald's voice had gone cool and cautious.

"I want help getting Hamilton back. If he is the only prisoner they have left." She swallowed bile at the back of her throat as she thought of Pim Wat cutting down the brave men who had set off on the mission. *Thom Tang . . .* her eyes teared up.

"We've had a clear directive from Washington not to get involved with any kind of direct confrontation. What is this deal you want to make?"

"I've got a prisoner. A woman with all the information you'll ever want about the Yām Khûmkạn. A woman who's also a mass murderer. My mother, Pim Wat."

"Whoa." A long silence as McDonald digested this. "You've captured her?"

"Indeed, I have."

"That's quite a bargaining chip." McDonald was stalling.

"Well. If you don't want this deal, I'm sure the Master will be interested in making an exchange for Hamilton."

"Not until we debrief her," McDonald said quickly.

"I'll allow that. And, when you do, I hope you will be using your most invasive interviewing techniques."

McDonald gave a bark of laughter. "I wouldn't want to get on your bad side, Sophie. Let me run this up the chain, but I am pretty confident my superiors will just about wet themselves for a chance to get their hands on your mother. I take it she hasn't endeared herself to you?"

"Killing my friends and stealing my child has cooled my affection, yes."

"And you haven't even heard Jake's harrowing tale of being tortured to death by her yet."

"What?" Sophie's voice went shrill.

"Yep. They managed to resuscitate him, but he spent longer than any of us want to on the Other Side. I'll let him tell you the story." The man harrumphed. "We definitely will want a crack at interviewing Pim Wat about the Yām Khûmkạn, but I can't promise we can make an exchange."

"Then the Master will be getting her. Or, I can dispose of her myself." *And it was absolutely the truth.* Sophie would have no problem sticking a blade into her mother and burying her somewhere deep and dark where she would never be found. But in fairness, she should let Armita do the honors . . .

"As I said, I'll get back to you right away," McDonald said.

"What's the number for the satellite phone you gave Jake? I need to reach him." Sophie was proud of how well she controlled the wobble in her voice.

McDonald's rattled off the digits, and Sophie recorded them mentally.

When she got off the phone with McDonald, Sophie's hands were shaking—and it wasn't at the idea of killing her mother.

CHAPTER THIRTY-FOUR

Day Twenty-Eight

JAKE WOKE to the electronic bleeping of the phone beside his bed as he swam up through the murky layers of the father of all hangovers.

"Shit." He tossed something off of him—and his eyes widened as that something murmured to him in Thai, stroking his chest and tugging at his hair. Jake sat up and groaned, clutching his head. "Oh *shit*."

The slender bronzed arms of one of the hookers he'd met in the bar the night before clutched at him. He looked over.

Ugh.

There were *two* of them. Noting his lack of interest, they turned to each other, kissing and cuddling.

Yeah, that had been a good time.

Self-disgust added to the foul brew in his belly.

He'd taken out his angst on some willing flesh that had no agenda about him but the bottom line—and it had felt great, just like finishing off the bottle of cheap Scotch tipped over on the sideboard.

And now, the party was over.

He squinted at the windows—blackout drapes cast the room into dimness, but bright bars of light around the edges indicated a day well underway.

"Thank you, ladies. Time to go." Jake made shooing motions. He reached for the phone which had mercifully gone silent—*Unknown Number.*

"Oh shit. Shit." *It had to be Sophie.* McDonald must have given her this number. He should have called her yesterday; he just couldn't get up the nerve to do what he needed to.

An incoming text dinged as one of the ladies, swaying her hips saucily and dressed in a whole lot of nothing, made her way to the coffeepot in the corner of the room while the other tried to massage his head.

He pushed the woman away. "No, thank you. We're done here. Cash is by the door." He'd had the presence of mind to put it there last night, hoping they'd leave before morning.

The text was from McDonald. *"Please contact Ms. Smithson. She wants to trade her mother for Hamilton. We can't help her get him out, but we want Pim Wat—so stall her and keep her from contacting the Master. We're going to get Pim Wat once we know where she's being held."* McDonald had helpfully included Sophie's private number.

"Son of a bitch!" He looked up from the phone and glared. "Why are you still here?"

The women twittered and giggled, but they weren't leaving. They pointed at the cash, shook their heads. Struck poses, blocking the door with their naked bodies. *They wanted more money.*

What a mess. Jake grabbed his wallet and pulled out all of the remaining *baht* McDonald had given him. "Ladies, thanks for the good times, but you need to go. I'm going to take a shower, and I want to be alone when I get out." He thrust the money at the one who'd made the coffee. "That's all I got."

Jake took his phone and the empty wallet into the bathroom with him—not that there was anything left to steal—his credit cards and ID were back at Connor's house on Phi Ni, left there as a precaution and not needed on their jungle mission. He locked the door, groaning again as he fumbled in the toiletry basket for some aspirin.

There was none to be found. Well, a sore head was no more than he deserved. He cursed, turned on the water as hot as it would go, and got into the shower.

Jake scrubbed his skin with a washcloth and soap until he burned from head to toe. Then he turned on the cold and stood under it until he was blue. Tipping his head back to let the water run straight into his mouth, Jake drank as much water as he could hold.

And then, he puked it up.

God, the misery. Almost as bad as being waterboarded to death.

Jake drank more water and repeated his hot/cold/scrubbing.

He had to get their touch off him.

He'd never resorted to hookers in his life before last night. *A new personal low.* He hated himself for sleeping with them, and yet he wasn't sorry.

He'd been betrayed. He didn't owe Sophie anything but a "good-bye, and here's why."

So why was he still so totally miserable? Because Sophie wouldn't know he'd had his cheap revenge with booze and hookers? *He could always tell her.* After all, it was honesty he was after. He gagged again, but nothing came up.

"Ugh! Why didn't I just fuckin' die in that torture room! Damn it!" Jake punched the tiled wall of the shower, and the pain did more to sober him up than his homegrown water treatment had.

Time to man up.

He got out. Dried off. Wrapped in a towel. Opened the door and peered out cautiously.

"Thank you, God." *Not that God had anything to do with the current fiasco . . .*

The hookers had gone, leaving nothing but the smell of perfume and sex behind. *Ugh, again.*

He stalked across the room and cranked up the air conditioning to clear out the funk, poured himself a Styrofoam cup of coffee, and called Room Service for breakfast and aspirin.

After he'd shaved, dressed, eaten, and swallowed the hotel's aspirin with a whole pot of coffee, Jake picked up his phone and called Sophie's number.

CHAPTER THIRTY-FIVE

Day Twenty-Eight

MALEE WAS CHANGING MOMI, cooing over her grand-niece as she diapered the infant in a spot of sunlight by the window, as Sophie set a bowl of steaming noodles down in front of Pim Wat.

"I don't know how you expect me to eat this with my hands tied behind my back," Pim Wat complained.

"I'm sure you can kill with just a spoon," Sophie said. "We're not taking any chances, Mother."

"I'll feed you." Armita, her eyes cold as a dead fish, approached Pim Wat.

The satellite phone rang.

"Are you sure?" Sophie cut her eyes to the phone. Jake's number lit the screen.

"I'm sure." Armita held a pair of chopsticks like they were a dagger. "I'll make sure she gets what she needs."

"All right." Sophie snatched up the phone. "I need privacy for this call."

She took the phone into the bedroom and shut the door, falling back against it and sucking in a breath for courage. She punched the On button.

"Jake! Are you all right?" Sophie put a hand to her throat, steadying her squeaky tone. "I was so worried!"

Jake cleared his throat. "I've been better." His voice sounded raspy.

"You're safe. That's all that matters." Sophie walked across the room to her cousin's sumptuously draped bed and got on top of it, folding her legs into lotus position. "I got Momi back! Armita stole her from Pim Wat and messaged me."

"That's great! How's the little bean doing?" They'd called Sophie's baby that, all through the pregnancy. Tender memories of that time thickened Sophie's throat, and she had to clear it to answer.

"Momi is fine. Thriving and putting on weight, actually. Armita took good care of her. And yesterday, we captured Pim Wat."

"Yeah, McDonald sent me a text." Jake's voice had gone remote again. "I'm sure that was an interesting situation."

"Jake. Why didn't you call me the minute you had access to a phone?" Sophie's voice was a cry of anguish. "I was frantic!"

"Some things happened in the compound."

"McDonald told me you almost died. I'm so sorry." Sophie waited, rubbing the scar that ran up her cheekbone, but he didn't say anything more. "He also told me Pim Wat killed everyone but you and Hamilton," she prompted.

"Yes. It was . . . bad. I've seen some things in my time, and what your mother did was right up there with war crimes."

"I'm so sorry." Sophie's eyes stung. "Thom Tang—Rhinehart. I can't imagine."

"Pim Wat had me tortured to death. I died, Sophie." Jake sighed, heavily.

"What happened?" Sophie could hardly bear to ask. "How are you still here?"

"Connor and the man they call the Master revived me." Jake cleared his throat again. "I'd been drowned in a tub of dirty water.

Not a good way to go. My lungs and throat are still a little wonky."

"That evil bitch!" Sophie balled her fists. "I'm planning to try to bargain with the CIA to trade Pim Wat for Hamilton. Regardless, my mother will never breathe free air again."

"Hamilton. Now there's an interesting situation." Jake's voice had gone silky, casual. "Did you know the guy has blue eyes? And blond hair?"

Sophie went very still. Her hand massaged the scar on her cheekbone. Her mouth worked, but nothing came out.

"Without his glasses, contacts and hair dye, Hamilton, or Connor, as he tells me his first name is, bears a striking resemblance to your old boyfriend, Todd Remarkian. I don't know how you've kept all those identities straight. Downright confusing for a poor jarhead like me."

"Oh, Jake." Sophie shut her eyes, rubbed them. "I wanted to tell you. He wouldn't let me."

"And you had to listen to him?" Jake's voice rose. "You had to lie to me? Choose loyalty to *him* over me?"

"It wasn't like that. It . . ." Her throat worked. "It wasn't my secret to tell. There were reasons. Big reasons."

"Don't worry, Sophie, the Ghost is out of the bag. I outed your boyfriend to the CIA. McDonald is collaborating with your FBI friend Marcella to put a case together. It's all going to come out in the wash, as they say. If Connor, or whatever his name is, ever gets out of the Yām Khûmkạn compound, he'll have a cell waiting for him."

"What have you done?" Sophie unwound her legs, stood up. She paced back and forth, tugging at handfuls of her hair. "Oh, Jake! Connor does good in the world! What have you done?"

"This is what's always been there. The bomb I was waiting for." Jake blew out a breath. "I knew it was too good to be true, that you chose me, that we were together. There was something off about Hamilton, but I didn't have all the pieces. I just couldn't put it all together. Then, when we were on the mission and captured, I thought Connor . . . was a friend. I tried to save him from torture, tried to help him." Jake's pain throbbed in his words. "And all along, you two were together. Conspiring. Keeping secrets. Were you sleeping with him?"

"No. It wasn't like that." Sophie raised her voice. *He had to believe her!* "Yes, I knew who Connor was, but he betrayed me when he faked the Todd Remarkian death. It killed my trust, killed my feelings for him. He tried to win me back, I'll grant you that, but it was you, Jake, *you* that I chose." Tears that felt as thick as oil welled in her eyes. "Don't make me regret that choice."

"I already do. Did you read my letter? Look at the box I left you on the bedside table?"

Sophie shut her eyes. "I did not. I was too upset about you both marooning me on the island. I just wanted to focus on getting Momi back. I'm sorry."

"Don't be sorry." Jake's voice strengthened. "I'm glad you didn't read my sniveling protestations of love. When you get back to the island, throw that letter in the shredder, will you? But mail me back the ring—I'm going to our Big Island office from here, so you can send it to me there. It's my grandmother's ring, and my mom will want it back."

Sophie's voice caught in a sob. "Really? After all we've been through? This is how it ends?"

"Yep. This is how it ends. But here's something to make it easier for you—I slept with two hookers last night, and drank a fifth of Scotch. I don't regret a thing." Jake ended the call.

Sophie collapsed on the bed, muffling her weeping into her cousin's pillow.

CHAPTER THIRTY-SIX

Day Twenty-Eight

SOPHIE DUG her way into her cousin's bed and buried herself under the covers. A stretch of dim and horribly painful time went by. The depression's jaws clamped down on her shredded throat, and she didn't even try to fight it.

Eventually, she felt her aunt's hand on her shoulder. "Sophie. Whatever is going on, your daughter needs you."

Momi's wails penetrated the fog that had settled over Sophie. She took the child into her nest of covers, cuddling and soothing her, but Momi arched and fought, inconsolable.

"She seems colicky," Armita said from the doorway. "I had to get a different brand of formula this time, and it doesn't seem to agree with her."

"I've put out the word we're looking for a wet nurse," Malee said. "I think human milk would be best for her. In the meantime, I ran a bath for you two in our big whirlpool tub. The hot water might help."

"Where's Pim Wat?" Sophie could barely open her swollen eyes.

"Tied up and secure," Armita said. "Did you think we'd let her get away? I'll kill her myself, first. Come, Sophie. Get in the bath. You and your baby can cry together in there, if it makes you feel better."

Sophie gave a wet chuckle. "Jake and I broke up."

"Your boyfriend? Oh dear, that's too bad," Malee murmured, but her eyes were on her phone. "He's not much of a gentleman, dumping you at a vulnerable time like this."

"It's complicated . . ." Tears welled in Sophie's eyes again. Momi howled, drowning her words.

"You don't need a man," Armita said. "We can take care of our girl just fine without a penis in our midst."

Clearly, the women in Sophie's life weren't sympathetic to her broken heart.

Sophie got out of bed, holding her crying baby close, and followed Armita into her aunt's palatial bathroom. A huge sunken tub awaited, gently steaming. Armita helped Sophie by taking the baby so she could disrobe, then handing Sophie the naked child once she was safely settled on the tub's built-in seat.

Momi blinked her tightly shut eyes as the warm water touched her skin. She flailed in reflex, arching to howl again. Sophie tucked her arms in close, pressing her baby against her chest. She sank a little deeper into the water, so only Sophie's shoulders and Momi's head were not submerged.

Gradually, the child began to relax. "There you are, my darling, beautiful girl. Hello. Does your tummy hurt? Oh, my dear, my tummy hurts too. So does my heart." Sophie kissed and snuggled the infant, and Momi's plump, pink mouth suckled at her wet skin.

Sophie suddenly remembered her dream—*that dream she'd had of nursing her child in the bath!* Her milk had let down just from the dream. What a bizarre déjà vu! Sophie moved to the shallower end of the bath, and offered her breast. Momi clamped on, giving a happy little grunt. Sophie bit her tongue on a gasp of pain. She gazed down at Momi's contented face and felt, miracle of miracles, the powerful sensation of her milk letting down.

"Oh, my dear one." Tears rose in Sophie's eyes yet again—*she was living the dream she'd had, a dream that had sustained her.* Her grief over Jake and the lurking depression receded as feel-good hormones flooded her system.

Her daughter was her priority.

She shut her eyes and felt nothing but blissful, pure, maternal love—until her breast ran dry a moment later, and Momi growled in frustration. "Yes, darling, we're going to have to work up to a full meal for you out of these poor dried-up things," she murmured, and put her daughter on the other side.

LATER, with Momi down for a nap, Sophie called her aunt and nanny into the dining room. Freshly dressed, her hair brushed out, Sophie was up and moving and she planned to stay that way. "We need a plan. A strategy. Jake is out of my life for now, so I'll be going forward alone. We can't let the Master get Pim Wat back—she's too dangerous, and there's no doubt in my mind that she'll come after us if she ever gets loose. I want you, Malee, to monitor her phone. The Master will eventually call her. How long was she visiting you for?"

"She didn't say. But Pim Wat usually swoops in on me for three to five days." Malee rubbed coconut oil into her bruised throat as she spoke. "He's only called once, that I'm aware of, when she had stayed a week."

"Good. That gives us a little time. Where is her phone? I need to get his number. I know I told McDonald that I wanted them to make a trade for me, but I'm virtually sure they won't help us get Connor back."

"Why do you need to get Connor back?" Armita's triangular face and uplifted brows expressed a certain mulish annoyance. "I think you might be better off with a completely fresh start from these men in your life."

"Hamilton is very important to me—and to our company, Security

Solutions, for reasons I can't go into right now. I owe him a lot for trying to get Momi back for me—in fact, I owe a debt to all the men who gave their lives to that mission." Sophie blew out a shaky breath. "I have to try to get him returned. I have the advantage of already knowing what the Master wants me to do—give bone marrow for the crown prince. I will negotiate Connor's release in trade for that."

"Doing the donation is a good thing," Malee agreed. "Our cousin is only a child."

"I would do it for that reason alone," Sophie said. "The proposed trade is just a way to get Hamilton back, but the Master doesn't have to know that. Give me Mother's phone. I need to get into it to obtain the Master's number."

Sophie plugged the phone into her laptop and used one of her decryption programs to unlock her mother's phone password. The whole enterprise took about five minutes.

Armita peered over her shoulder as Sophie scrolled through the numbers on the phone. "The Master" was listed under *Favorites*.

"I was hoping to find out his real name," Sophie said.

"Everyone in the Yām Khûmkạn gives up his name. They get a number, and a designation. They no longer hold their former identities," Armita said.

Sophie frowned. "In all my research about the Yām Khûmkạn, I couldn't find out even that basic fact."

"There is no substitute for in-person espionage," Armita said. "Lack of individuality is another layer of anonymity for their agents, as well as a tool to bond the men to the cause."

Sophie cocked a brow. "You have definitely added to your skill set and knowledge base." She patted her former nanny's arm. "I am so glad that you will be here, helping me raise Momi. Now that I have the Master's contact information, I just have to call the CIA back and see if they have decided about helping me negotiate Connor's release. If they have, I will let them take the lead with the Yām Khûmkạn. If they have not . . ."

"In any case, you should call the baby's father and let him know Momi is safe," Armita said. "He deserves that."

A twist of guilt cramped Sophie's belly. "Of course. That was next on my list."

How had she somehow forgotten that Alika was a player in her child's life? She had been so focused on getting the baby back, on bonding with her child again, that she had forgotten she shared Momi with him, and his family. And her own father, too!

She would have to figure out how sharing Momi with Alika could work. She had planned to stay on Phi Ni Island for the immediate future, to conduct negotiations for Connor's release, and resume Security Solutions business from there.

She was definitely not going back to her apartment on the Big Island. Right now, she couldn't be in the same building as Jake, let alone working closely with him at that extension office.

Those days were over.

Sophie refused to cry any more over the breakup. He had made his choice, and it was to walk away from her. She stood by her decision not to tell him Connor's identity—it hadn't been her secret to tell. She'd never been unfaithful to Jake, and if he couldn't believe that, it was his problem.

Some part of her wasn't even surprised—she had always been braced for the moment when Jake reached his limit with the secrets that surrounded her. *But it didn't make it hurt less.*

Refreshing her tea, Sophie sat down and called Alika on the secure satellite phone. He was shocked to hear that she and Jake had broken up. "What? No way."

"It was Jake's choice. There were secrets I kept from him for reasons that he doesn't understand. But I don't want you to blame him," Sophie said. "I don't blame him." As she spoke the words, she knew they were true. "We all have deal breakers, as Marcella calls them. Jake discovered one, with me."

"Your relationship is none of my business," Alika said, with deliberate calm. "But my daughter *is* my business. And I want Momi safe, and back in the United States as soon as possible."

Sophie wasn't ready to return—there was too much to do here. "I understand why you feel that way. It's just that things are so unsettled right now. We will have to cross that bridge when we come to it, Alika, and figure out an arrangement that works for both of us. But for the short term, can you plan to come visit us here in Thailand, as soon as I know where we'll be?"

Alika breathed audibly. He must be frantic to see his daughter again, and Sophie appreciated that he was trying not to be controlling or possessive. "I'll be on the next plane out the minute you give me the word. Please keep me posted. I'm sure my mom and Tutu will want to come as well."

"They'd be welcome. I'm planning to go back to . . . the place where I was before." She didn't want to name Phi Ni aloud; and she still had concerns that the Yām Khûmkạn might have pried its location out of Connor. Sophie sighed, staring out her aunt's window to where a brightly colored bird drank from the garden fountain. "Thank you for being so steady for me through all of this. Have you had any more troubles from the police?"

"No. Detective Jenkins will be glad to hear you and our girl are reunited, I'm sure." Alika sighed too. "I can't wait to see our baby. Thank you for being the incredible warrior that you are, getting our daughter back."

"A warrior. Yes, I like that. Momi has the best of both of us." She'd always loved that Alika believed in her, reveled in her competence, and never doubted her. Nothing Sophie did threatened his masculinity. Even when she had beaten him in the MMA ring, he'd found her sexy and attractive.

Such different dynamics with each of the men she'd loved—Connor had enjoyed her online skills and competing with her in cat and mouse games; Jake had needed to beat her in the ring at first, but had come to be a true partner with time. Alika had been a mentor, a teacher, and a true friend. *Now she had none of them.*

As if reading her mind, Alika cleared his throat. "Since you told me about Jake . . . I think I should let you know that Sandy and I are dating."

"Sandy? Your physical therapist?" Sophie had been impressed with the attractive blonde double amputee when she met her.

"Yep." His voice was upbeat; he sounded happy. "Obviously, I'm not her client any more. But we found we have a lot in common, and we're enjoying spending time together."

Sandy, a former medic and Afghanistan IED explosion survivor, was a perfect match for Alika with her athleticism and helping profession. She wouldn't endanger him as Sophie had. Sophie squelched a twinge of possessive jealousy as she thought of the woman becoming a family with Alika and her child. *Time enough to adjust to that as it unfolded.* "Don't put the cart before the horse," Marcella would say.

"I'm so glad for you, Alika. You deserve every happiness." She meant it sincerely.

"You, too, Soph. Don't give up. Things have a way of resolving in unexpected and perfect ways."

"You're always so positive. I struggle more with the dark side of things. But I'm finding our daughter to be a great antidote for that. It even looks like I might be able to breastfeed her after all." Sophie wrapped up the conversation after sending him a phone photo of their sleeping baby.

The next call Sophie made was to McDonald at the CIA. As she had been concerned he would, he told her that the agency could not get involved with her negotiations for Connor. "But we want Pim Wat."

"What can the CIA do to help me get Connor back?" Sophie asked harshly. "I'm not giving you something for nothing."

"We will be there as backup in the Yām Khûmkạn's territory. The minute Connor is released, we will fetch him. We'll keep both of you safe, in any attempts at an exchange. We just can't go on the offensive on behalf of a single citizen."

"Not just a single citizen. Seven of our men and their guide were cut down in cold blood, unless you have forgotten them already," Sophie said angrily. "I want you to locate their bodies in that mass grave in the jungle. Get the bodies back to their families."

McDonald seemed to be thinking that over. "We can do that," he said at last. "I can also stand by while you call the Master to negotiate for Connor. I can lend the backup weight of the U.S. Government to your negotiations."

"An empty offer and an excuse to listen in on me. No, thank you. I've seen how long it takes for you to make any decisions or take any action."

"I'm sorry if it seems that way. We have protocols, because quick action often has unintended consequences. That said—let us take Pim Wat off your hands. She's a dangerous security risk and could impede your negotiations with the Master if he finds out you have her. What is your location?"

The responsibility of keeping her mother prisoner when the Master might come looking for her with his ninja armies was a little bit terrifying.

Sophie gave the address of her aunt's house. "I prefer to reach out to the Master after you pick up my mother. I don't want to take the chance that he can trace my contact, and come after my location."

"I'll be there within the hour," McDonald said, and ended the call.

Sophie got up and went into the living room, where Malee and Armita were playing with Momi. Both women looked up. "She had a good nap," Armita said. "I weighed her, and she's gaining, which is good. She's up two hundred grams."

"Good. I guess the combo of breast milk and formula agrees with her." Sophie put her hands on her hips. "You two need to figure out a way to get to Hamilton's island, Phi Ni, without being detected. Work on that, while I go talk to Mother."

CHAPTER THIRTY-SEVEN

Day Twenty-Eight

Pɪᴍ Wᴀᴛ ᴛᴇsᴛᴇᴅ ʜᴇʀ ʙᴏɴᴅs. She'd been doing that since she'd been captured two days ago, flexing her hands against the duct tape Armita had wrapped her extremities in. So far, she hadn't been able to get the tape to move. Armita had duct-taped her feet, too, but later had to cut that off and substitute rope since they moved her back and forth between the houses with a pillowcase on her head, so she couldn't see where she was and fight back.

Fight back and kill all three of the foul demons who'd betrayed her: daughter, sister, beloved maid. She entertained herself with a fantasy of how she would kill each of them.

Drowning. Electrocution. Suffocation. Poison. A razor blade. Or burning . . . the possibilities were endless, but the process would definitely be slow. And painful.

The floor of the storage shed Pim Wat lay upon in her former home was filthy, and dark as a cave. The duct tape over her lips itched against her skin, and her mouth was dry. She wriggled, trying to find a comfortable position on the gritty cement floor, but there was none to be had when lying on her side with her arms bound behind her back.

They were doing this to punish her, to give her a taste of what she'd doled out to Sophie's men, and to them, each in different ways. Pim Wat understood that. But she wouldn't forgive it.

What they didn't know was that she'd trained under the Master. She was inured to cold, hunger, and pain. She could go into a little room in her mind and spend time there with pleasant memories that released endorphins, buffering her against the discomfort of temporary circumstances.

She settled into what was the best possible position given her limited options, shut her eyes, and went into a calm place more restorative than sleep.

Hours passed. Maybe days.

The screech of the old wooden door against the floor was actually a rude awakening from the sleepy trance into which Pim Wat had sent herself. She opened her eyes reluctantly, recognizing Sophie's tall outline. She lay quietly as Sophie undid the restraint on her feet.

"I will take you to use the bathroom and get you some water. And then, we will talk," her daughter said.

This was the first time Sophie had addressed her directly since she'd knocked Pim Wat out with her gun and Pim Wat had woken up a captive. Sophie had avoided her, delegating her care and handling to Malee and Armita. Perhaps it was because she felt guilty for treating her mother so barbarically?

Hopefully that was the case. Guilt was an emotion she could use.

Pim Wat cooperated as Sophie led her to the bathroom—all part of her strategy. Her lack of resistance was confusing to the other women; they expected her to fight and thrash, to provide them with opportunities to hurt her. *She was too smart for that.* She would be soft and sweet, use her big eyes to beg, and when they least expected it, when they gave her an opportunity, she would strike.

The Master had given her a gift, identifying her with the cobra.

Malee was the weakest of the three, the most conflicted about her sister's captivity. She hadn't seen the things the other women described Pim Wat to have done; she only knew Pim Wat's constant bullying, the little ways Pim Wat had liked to see her suffer but had learned to conceal as they grew up.

Armita would definitely kill her given half a chance.

But Sophie? She wasn't sure. *Perhaps she still had leverage with her daughter.*

Pim Wat stumbled on the stairs to test the theory—and scraped her knee severely when Sophie failed to catch or support her. She let easy tears well in her eyes and run down her face, catching on the sacrilege of duct tape over her mouth.

"Crocodile tears, I've heard those called," Sophie said, hoisting Pim Wat up roughly. "Get moving. We're on a schedule."

Pim Wat did her business on the house's old toilet with Sophie standing guard over her. Her daughter tipped her forward and wiped for her—all with the expression of a robot, a withdrawn coldness that she'd never had when young.

Assan Ang had taught her that face, and Pim Wat felt an unwelcome stab of regret. She'd never meant that marriage to be a bad thing for Sophie. Such a shame; Ang had ruined her sweet, biddable girl and made her into this hard, formidable woman—*as the Master had done for her.* Maybe they had more in common than it seemed . . .

Sophie brought Pim Wat into the empty house's living room area and tied her to one of the dining room chairs. Pim Wat tested the ropes; they were tight but not inhumane.

Sophie ripped the tape off Pim Wat's mouth, eliciting a cry. *That adhesive hurt!* Pim Wat licked fresh blood from her lip, unable to wipe it off. "How can you treat me like this?"

"You're playing the victim. None of us is fooled."

"I'm your mother!"

"Don't remind me." Sophie's clearly marked brows drew down, and with her hands on her hips, she looked just like her father, Frank, when he was getting ready to give Pim Wat "a piece of his mind" as he used to call it. "I should treat you as you treated the men who went after my infant daughter—to rescue her from *you*, I might add. Brave, good men with families—and you gutted and decapitated them." Sophie leaned down into Pim Wat's face and spit on it. "That's how I feel about you. Death is too good for you."

Pim Wat blinked in astonishment—*her daughter really hated her!* She wiped the spittle from her face as best she could by rubbing it on her shoulder. "Insolent bitch."

"The only reason you're alive at all is that I hope the CIA has a rough interrogation plan for you, and a long incarceration without possibility of due process." Sophie tugged a chair over and sat down facing her mother. "Let's clear the air, shall we? You stole my daughter from me when she was twelve hours old. Why?"

"I thought the baby might be a match for the crown prince's bone marrow." Pim Wat shrugged, but embarrassment heated her neck. *Saying these things aloud sounded bad.* "We were going to take you, but you delivered earlier than scheduled. Momi was easier to move than you would have been. I'm sure Armita told you all of this."

"And when Momi wasn't a match?" Pink stained Sophie's tawny cheeks as she flushed with emotion. "You kept my daughter anyway. With not even a word to me. Didn't even offer any kind of deal or ransom—you just *stole* her."

"What can I say? I wanted a 'do-over' as they say in America." Pim Wat tilted her head, eyeing Sophie. "I discovered that I had . . . regrets. About you. About our relationship. And Momi is a pretty baby. She will grow up to be a beautiful woman. As you were, before that scar ruined your face."

Sophie clapped a hand to the cheek that had been rebuilt with prosthetics and a skin graft. "Oh, you are so cruel, Mother! It makes it easier for me to hand you over to people who will not treat you gently."

"I was only speaking the truth. People can't handle the truth."

Pim Wat shook her head. "I will always be your mother. I gave you life. That is the truth, and you owe me for that."

"No, Mother. I paid that debt in blood, long ago." Sophie rose to her feet. "I just wanted to have this little chat and tell you, so you can think about it, that all of this death and drama was unnecessary. I would have come to Thailand, gone to a hospital, and donated bone marrow for the Prince—if you'd only asked me." Sophie's honey-brown gaze bored into Pim Wat's. "You assume everyone is like you and needs to be coerced. Some of us still have a conscience, and simple compassion, especially for children." Sophie blew out a breath. "I, too, have regrets about our relationship. I regret all the love, care, and obedience I gave you, without question, for so many years." Sophie picked up the roll of duct tape resting on the counter and ripped off a piece. "Any last words, Mother?"

"I'm sorry, Sophie Malee." Pim Wat's eyes welled up, and she wasn't in control of the wetness that spilled over to run down her cheeks. "I am not like other people, the Master tells me—but knowing you makes me wish that I was."

"Thanks for the apology," Sophie said. "I accept it on behalf of the men you killed. And it changes nothing."

The tape sealed Pim Wat's mouth, but she had nothing more to say, anyway.

The increasing *whump whump whump* sound of an approaching helicopter made Sophie hurry to undo the ropes binding Pim Wat to the chair. "Your time with us has come to an end, Mother."

Fear cast a chill over Pim Wat for the first time, and so did regrets that she couldn't name, couldn't explain, and could do nothing about. "My, how the mighty have fallen," her sister had mocked her, yesterday in the garden. "You get to go to prison and be tortured, just like you've done to so many others."

Tears continued to soak the tape on Pim Wat's face. Her body felt like lead. Her heart beat with heavy thuds. What was this? Grief? *What a strange and terrible feeling . . .* Sophie tugged Pim Wat, feet dragging, through the house and toward the steep flight of exterior stairs leading down from the upper story.

"Come on. The CIA doesn't have all day." Sophie held Pim Wat's arm in one hand, and the banister in the other—and tugged her forward. "Let's go."

The CIA.

Guantánamo.

Torture lay ahead, regret lay behind.

Pim Wat pitched forward, her arm wrenching out of Sophie's grip.

Maybe she even jumped—*did it matter?*

She fell with a cry that never escaped, trapped by the tape on her mouth—but that scream echoed in her mind as she felt the hard edge of the steep wooden step as it came up to meet her helpless, bound body.

Pim Wat bounced down the stairs, every sharp edge biting into soft flesh and breaking bones. She felt every crushing blow dealt by inertia and gravity until the very last step, at the bottom.

CHAPTER THIRTY-EIGHT

Day Twenty-Eight

ARMITA HELD the baby close against her shoulder. Momi's warm weight felt like both an anchor and a buoy, lifting her and holding her in place at the same time. She rubbed the infant's back, murmuring softly into the tiny pink ear.

Her eyes tracked the two CIA agents as they carefully loaded Pim Wat's body onto a sturdy garden lattice Malee had hastily removed from the house and covered with towels.

Her former mistress was still alive, but barely. Pim Wat looked small and broken lying there on the makeshift stretcher, her face an unrecognizable mess of blood and long black hair. Armita watched Sophie cover her mother gently with a comforter from the house as a large older white man directed the agents in loading the makeshift stretcher onto the helicopter, parked in a vacant lot on the other side of Malee's house.

Had Pim Wat jumped? Had Sophie pushed her? Or had she merely tripped, as was so dangerous with one's hands behind her back?

No one would know the real answer to that but Sophie and her mother.

Malee approached, her face swollen from crying, her cheeks shiny with tears. "Give me the baby. I don't want her frightened by the noise from the helicopter."

Armita let the child go reluctantly. Malee hurried into the house clutching the baby tightly, and closed its bright, painted door.

All three of them drew comfort from Momi through these difficult times. Caring for the infant felt like caring for their own hurt inner children.

What a strange insight to have while watching her once-beloved mistress be taken away, quite possibly dying. Armita felt nothing but relief—perhaps she would die, and then Pim Wat's venomous presence would be gone from the world.

Armita shut her eyes and wished death on Pim Wat.

Sophie was speaking to the man she called McDonald. The blustery agent gestured with his hands. He pointed to the stretcher and tossed his hands skyward, clearly frustrated that his captive spy had almost fallen to her death. Sophie shook her head, shrugged her shoulders, and turned and walked back to Armita.

Her former ward's face was expressionless, unlike her aunt Malee's had been.

Life had not been kind to Sophie. She had learned inscrutability to protect herself, but the suppression of her emotions cost her dearly.

The two women stood side by side, shoulders almost touching, as the stretcher was secured in the helicopter with the doors open for it to fit. Once they'd stowed Pim Wat securely, McDonald clambered on board.

The chopper's rotors began their heavy *whop whop whop*. The sound increased, the helicopter's roar eliminating everything else. Sophie and Armita withdrew, heading into Sophie's former home.

They ascended the steep exterior wooden stairs that had so

recently claimed a victim. When they reached the living area, Armita turned to Sophie. "Are you all right?"

"I don't know. I still can't tell if she tripped, or if she jumped. In any case, I did not mean for that to happen." Sophie's impassive mask slipped. Her lips trembled. Her eyes were haunted. "Maybe I did push her. I just don't know."

Armita had half of her answer. "Will she live?"

"I don't know that either. She was still alive, but barely—that head injury seemed severe, and she was barely breathing. One of the agents had some medical training and he looked her over but didn't have much of an idea what was going on. Her cheekbone and jaw were broken, judging by the way they were looking. I don't know if moving her will make her worse, or save her. But since the CIA was on their way, and emergency services being what they are out here—having them take her to the closest US treatment facility seemed best. McDonald will do all he can to keep her alive." Sophie rubbed her own damaged cheekbone, a habitual gesture. "I don't know whether I hope she lives or dies."

"You did the right thing." Armita squeezed Sophie's shoulder.

"I did the only thing." Sophie walked into the kitchen and poured them each a glass of water. "It's important to stay hydrated in times of stress, and I'm breastfeeding now." Sophie sipped, staring out the window over the overgrown yard.

Armita drained her glass too, feeling numb and heavy.

She was liberated at last from the control of a fickle, cruel mistress. So why was she so sad and conflicted? Because Pim Wat wasn't always horrible. Her beautiful mistress could be high-spirited and generous. Pim Wat had no one in her life but Armita and the Master—and in her twisted way, she loved them both.

Sophie set down her empty glass and turned back to Armita. "I want you here while I call the Master. I want you to help me figure out what to say to him. I do not want to give away any unnecessary information. He must have no idea what has happened to Pim Wat; if he finds out I had anything to do with her injury and capture by the

CIA . . . I don't know what he would do to Connor." Sophie's face was pale with stress. "I need to stay very focused and calm for this call."

Armita's heart rate picked up as Sophie's apprehension spread, but she had to stay strong for all of their sakes. Sophie really had no idea the extent of the power the Master wielded—he had massive influence with a number of world governments because he kept the sons of officials from all over the world at the compound, studying his arcana—as willing hostages.

While the Master did not seem the vengeful type, the man was absolutely cold when it came to achieving his objectives. Right now, that objective was obtaining Sophie's bone marrow. But how would he react to news of Pim Wat's injury and capture? Armita didn't want to find out.

"Get a pen and paper. Let's make some notes, develop a script for you. The Master is uncanny in his persuasiveness. You will find yourself telling him things you never would have intended to."

"That's exactly what I'm afraid of," Sophie said, and got out her tablet. "I'll make notes on this."

"How DID you get this number, Sophie Smithson?" The Master's rich voice, on speakerphone, filled the small bathroom the two women had crowded into to contain the sound, and so that Armita could monitor the conversation.

"You are not untraceable, sir. I am calling because you have something I want." Sophie's voice was steady, but tension bracketing her eyes revealed her stress. Armita patted her arm encouragingly.

"The man I released must have told you by now about the prince and his condition."

"He has."

"My offer is this: provide what the prince needs, and I will return your man to you. Provided, of course, that Connor wants to go."

Sophie frowned. "Why would he want to stay at the compound?"

"Connor has a taste for the deeper things. He has a wonderful mind and a great curiosity," the Master said.

Armita felt the appeal of the man's words, as Sophie must. "Don't hurt him," Sophie whispered.

Facing Sophie, Armita shook her head vigorously and made a throat-cutting gesture. But it was too late. The Master's voice was already casting its spell over Sophie—Armita could see it happening and could do nothing to stop it.

"Why would I do that? I enjoy a life of the mind, the spirit, and the body, and Connor does too. I think you have the wrong impression of me, based upon your mother and her behavior."

Sophie met Armita's eyes and cleared her throat. "Are you telling me that you had nothing to do with the ambush that took my men's lives?"

"That was most unfortunate. I left communications with you about the prince's bone marrow up to your mother. I should have known that she could not, or would not, exercise finesse. Much as I care for her, Pim Wat has a limited perspective."

Sophie nodded in agreement, clearly forgetting the Master could not see her gesture. "My mother is a psychopath."

"Be that as it may," the Master said imperturbably. "In this instance, she allowed her dark appetites an upper hand. I should not have given her free rein, and for that I apologize."

Armita's eyes widened involuntarily—this was the first time she'd *ever* heard the Master apologize.

She had to get them off the subject of Pim Wat! She had to keep Sophie focused before she let something slip. She picked up the tablet on which they'd made notes, picked up the stylus and underlined the sentence, *get specifics on the exchange.* She held the tablet up for Sophie to see.

Sophie nodded, and continued her conversation with the Master. "While I find talking with you interesting, we must stay on topic. Where shall I go to make the bone marrow donation? And before you tell me I need to come to the compound, I refuse to go there. I will, however, go somewhere public and medically focused, like a hospital. That's all I will consider."

"I am glad to hear that, because your cousin is currently at Bangkok Hospital. Contact this doctor there." He rattled off a doctor's name and number. "He is coordinating the prince's care. Identify yourself as the prince's cousin Sophie Smithson. They will be expecting you."

"And after that? When are you releasing Connor?" Sophie's voice sounded raspy. Armita patted her arm again.

"I will be in touch, with a place and time for you to pick up your man."

"He's not my man."

"Oh no? Then whose is he?" The Master ended the call.

CHAPTER THIRTY-NINE

Day Thirty-Two

LATE EVENING SUNLIGHT slanted in as Jake opened the door of his studio apartment in Hilo. Memories assailed him as soon as he did so —mostly of how seldom he'd actually spent time in the sparsely decorated space. Sophie's apartment, a few doors down on the same floor, was bigger, with a separate bedroom that she used as a home office. They'd found her place to be a little more comfortable, with the spare room where their two large dogs could sprawl on their beds out from underfoot. They had both set up their futon beds to face the sliders that looked out over Hilo Bay, and Jake had spent most nights with Sophie in a room with a layout that mirrored this one.

His apartment smelled musty, unopened. Which of course, was exactly what it was. He had been gone for over a month.

Jake set down the backpack of necessities he had picked up in Thailand, but there was nothing in it of value but the laptop and new phone he had procured to replace those left at Connor's before the start of the mission. He walked across the carpet and opened the glass slider, going out onto the little deck to breathe in the wind off of the Bay.

If he shut his eyes, and just listened to the sound of the coqui frogs tuning up in the banyan tree, he could pretend they never left Hawaii. Pretend that the sun was setting on a busy day and Sophie and the baby were in her apartment, with the dogs. He was just grabbing a few things, a change of clothes, before heading over to her place for the night. He could pretend that he was still working on getting her to move to an actual house, where they could live together, building a life and a family, with his ring on her finger.

But that wasn't what was happening.

His misery needed a physical expression.

Jake turned and went into the workout corner he had set up, a simple rubber mat and a weight set and bench for when he was stuck at home for some reason. He sat down on the bench, picked up the barbell, and did overhead presses. Then lat pulldowns. And then, sit-ups on the slant board.

His body felt unfamiliar, a combination of both old and new—as if he had to learn everything all over again.

Maybe dying was some kind of cosmic reset button—the first day of the rest of his miserable life.

His phone toned, buzzing in a circle where he had set it on the counter when he entered. He got up and scowled when he saw the name on the little screen: Dr. Kinoshita, Security Solutions' psychologist. He'd known she would want a debrief, and that time must've come.

"Hey, Dr. Kinoshita. I know we need to talk. I'd like to set something up for tomorrow." Jake didn't let her ask him any questions. He got her to commit to a time for a Skype interview, and ended the call.

He didn't need to look around after setting down the phone to know that this apartment held nothing for him.

Tomorrow, he'd go work at the Hilo office and see what was on the schedule for investigation. He'd pick up the reins of his life and figure out how to go on. But for now, he needed a distraction. He didn't want to go through the decision tree that had led to breaking up with Sophie even one more time today.

Jake tied on his running shoes and headed out.

The sunset blazed to the west. Palm trees rustled in a gentle breeze. Yep, this was a tame and mellow paradise compared to the jungles of Thailand—and a brisk run around the park at Hilo Bay was just what the doctor ordered.

Jake ran too hard to think, blazing along the paved walkway past old ladies on park benches, tourists with cameras, mynah birds on palm trees. Every time he thought of Sophie, he stopped and did push-ups.

If push-ups worked as punishment for the recruits of the Yām Khûmkạn, they were good enough for him.

Making a formal statement to the police with Bix on Oahu had been a sobering exercise. He'd had to describe the men who had left on the ill-fated mission with them, the progress of their journey, and their bloody and fatal end. Reliving those moments of horror in detail had left him cold and shaky.

"Are you sure you're okay, Jake?" Bix hadn't wanted to let him leave Oahu so quickly to return to running the Big Island office alone. The President of Operations had let him go eventually, on the condition that he would speak to Dr. Kinoshita. If the psychologist gave Jake the all clear to work, he could get back into the office.

He didn't think Sophie would be coming back to the Big Island anytime soon. She wouldn't want to work with him in close proximity any more than he'd want to be near her, and Alika would want time with his daughter. She'd either end up on Kaua`i or Oahu.

Momi. Now there was a painful thought. He hadn't just lost Sophie, he'd lost the baby he'd chosen to think of as his daughter.

But she never had been.

Just as well that Jake had never been able to get to know her.

Jake dropped to the ground for more push-ups, besieged by unwelcome thoughts.

He just couldn't take any more of the lies and betrayals.

Secrets would always be a part of his life if he stayed with

Sophie. There would be things she wouldn't tell him. People she saw that he never knew about.

He'd gotten used to Alika being a part of the picture by truly believing that, in spite of Momi's existence, any romantic connection with Sophie was over.

But Connor was another story.

Connor still loved Sophie. And all this time, he'd likely been trying to get her back, trying to get her to forgive him for faking his death.

Connor was a major player. Who could resist a good-looking billionaire entrepreneur hacker dude with a private island? The man was perfect for Sophie, except for that one glaring problem—his addiction to vigilante justice. And honestly, Jake couldn't see that being that much of a problem after all they'd been through lately. Whether or not she had ever had sex with Connor while she was with Jake, she shared an emotional connection with the man, and he just couldn't tolerate it.

And Connor was his boss.

That was something else that needed to change. When the man came back from Thailand, Jake would quit the company. Leave this scuzzy apartment and move on with his life somewhere else. He'd done it before, and he could do it again—never mind how sick his stomach felt at the thought.

Jake cursed aloud. He'd promised himself he was done thinking about it, going through the loop again! *The push-ups weren't enough.* He jumped into some burpees, heaving his legs out so hard they tore holes in the grass, then jumping back up. Sweat poured into his eyes and blinded him.

"You okay, uncle?" A little mixed-Hawaiian girl stood in front of him, holding the leash of a shaggy dog that was much too big for her. "You get pilikia?"

Pilikia—the Hawaiian word for trouble. Yep, Jake had that in spades. He swiped his forehead with an arm. "Nah, kid. I'm fine. Just some problems at work." Jake smiled, but it hurt his face.

"You should drink water. There's some over there." The child pointed to a nearby water fountain. She was so cute, this little girl like so many in Hawaii—all big brown eyes, long black hair, warm brown skin. *She looked just like Momi would someday.*

Jake dusted off his hands. "I'm good, thanks. Have a nice day, kid. And remember not to talk to strangers—not everybody deserves your sweet smile, okay?"

She giggled. "Okay."

The dog spotted something more interesting than Jake, and towed the child away to investigate. Jake looked around for a parent. He finally spotted a chubby woman pushing a stroller and hollering for her daughter. He waved to her and pointed to the kid, and then moved off at a jog.

He forced himself to think about reentering the office and picking up his long-neglected cases.

Felicia would have things in order. She had kept the whole Big Island operation running while they were tied up with the birth and then the kidnapping.

That girl was a gem.

Jake ran back to the house, feeling better. Looser. A little more alert. He'd gotten a few endorphins going, he was on his way back to getting in shape, and he even had a plan: he'd find another security outfit to work for, maybe even leave Hawaii. There was work all over the world for someone with his skills.

Never mind that he'd been looking forward to letting that life-style go, and settling down with the woman he loved and their child.
. .

Jake jogged up the stairs to the third-floor landing, and pulled up short at the sight of Felicia standing outside his door. The pretty blonde was balancing an extra-large pizza on one hand, and holding a six-pack of beer in the other. She was staring at the door, clearly debating which to put down in order to ring his bell. She turned and smiled. Jake blinked at the radiance of her grin.

"Thought you might want a little welcome home party. I even

brought my collection of The Walking Dead DVDs for us to binge-watch."

An answering smile pulled Jake's cheeks up into an unfamiliar curve, and this time it didn't hurt. "That sounds perfect." He took in her cute figure dressed in her workout clothes—short shorts and a sleeveless tee. "You're a sight for sore eyes, babe."

"I told you not to call me that." Felicia's smile faded. "Unless you were asking me out."

"Sophie and I are not together anymore." *When would it stop hurting to say that?*

"What? Oh my God. I'm so sorry." Felicia's eyes widened. The pizza box tipped dangerously, headed for disaster.

Jake lunged forward and caught the box. "It's a long story, and it's not pretty. You got time? I need to practice my spiel for the debrief with Dr. Kinoshita, and I'd love to catch you up."

Felicia held up the six-pack. "What do you think this is for?"

"Then come on in." Jake grinned as he unlocked the door. "Babe."

Felicia shook her head. "Not funny, old man."

But it *was* kind of funny, and he was smiling—for the first time in days.

CHAPTER FORTY

Day Thirty-Three

THE CROWN PRINCE of Thailand gazed up at Sophie from a wheel-chair, his eyes circled by dark rings, his skin sallow and his lips ashy. He looked deeply ill, and Sophie's heart squeezed with compassion as she dropped to a height to take his hand. "My Prince, it's great to meet you. I'm your cousin Sophie. I have been living in the United States so we have not been able to meet before."

"My mother told me that. I am glad to meet you, as well." His hand felt chilly and limp in hers.

Six black-clad Yām Khûmkạn ninjas surrounded them. From the moment Sophie had shown up at the hospital, she had been surrounded by her own security detail of warriors. Clearly, the Yām Khûmkạn took their duties as guardians of the royal family seriously.

The heavyset woman who had been pushing the young prince's wheelchair came forward, and Sophie straightened up and hugged her cousin, careful not to touch her elaborate headdress. "I'm sorry it took me so long to get here to help, Your Majesty. I didn't know your son was sick."

"I told your mother at least two years ago that Bashar was having his first round of chemo," the queen said, frowning. "He has gone through multiple rounds, and it is in remission—but as you may have heard it can do, the treatment's wiped out his red blood cells. If this bone marrow transfer works, it could help rebuild his system."

"That's what I'm here for. Glad to help."

"Your mother told me that you have had a child," the queen said. "Congratulations!"

"Yes, I am very happy. I have a healthy daughter, Momi Tansanee. She is waiting for me, and that makes me eager to complete this process. I understand the whole procedure will take some time, and I will need a bit of recovery as well."

"We are so glad we were able to meet you here so the transmission can be immediate. I can't wait to see a little color bloom in my son's cheeks."

"Mama. You're embarrassing me," the prince complained.

Sophie shook her head, smiling. "My father still embarrasses me, Your Highness. Parents are just like that."

A tall ninja with long, braided black hair, unusual because the rest of the warriors had shaved heads, walked over to them. Taller than the rest of the black-clad guards, he wore a white *gi* and an aura of power. The queen inclined her head graciously as the man bowed from the waist, his hands folded. The prince smiled and extended a hand. "Master. You came."

"Of course. I'm here to watch over you and this procedure, Your Highness," the man said. Sophie took in the man's well-built figure, his glossy braid decorated with jade ornaments, the simple leather slip-ons he wore. He turned toward her. Sophie blinked, surprised by his dark purple eyes.

"Sophie Malee. Your mother speaks of you often. I am pleased to meet you at last." The man took her hand. His grip was cool and dry; hers was hot and sweaty.

Sophie nodded like a marionette, groping for words. "You must be the Master."

"Yes." His unusual gaze tracked over her face. "I see your beautiful mother in your face."

Sophie's chest flushed at the compliment, and her hand fluttered over the scar on her cheek. "You are too kind."

Her heart gave a twinge of guilt and sorrow. Pim Wat had disappeared into the bowels of the CIA's system, and she still didn't know whether her mother had lived or died. She had no idea what kind of care the agency had provided her—it would be as good as they were able to give, because they wanted her alive. But would it be good enough?

The warmth in the Master's unusual eyes told Sophie that he loved her mother.

He must never know what had happened to Pim Wat. The Master would make a formidable enemy.

A white jacketed doctor came in with a clipboard. "Sophie Smithson? We have some procedural things to go over with you."

Sophie turned back to the queen and the prince, and bowed. "I'm sure you have things to do to prepare as well. I am honored that I can help."

"Thank you, Sophie," the queen said. The prince inclined his head, looking exhausted.

"We want to go over the procedure with you," the doctor said. "Come this way, please."

Sophie caught the Master's pristine sleeve in her fingers. "Walk with me."

His eyes flashed with something—surprise? Resentment? Sophie had the feeling that not too many people touched or directed him as she had. He bowed to the royals, and followed Sophie as they went out into the hallway in the doctor's wake. Out in the hall, Sophie turned to face him. "I require proof of life before I go any further. Show me a photo or video, or preferably get Connor on the phone, so that I can verify he is alive and well."

"I anticipated you would want that. I have a timestamp video from this morning's surveillance feed at the compound." The Master drew a phone out of his pocket, and swiped to a video.

Sophie bent close to see, her heart rate speeding up as she searched the rows of practicing recruits for any sign of Connor. At last she spotted him where he stood at the back, taller than the rest, his white scalp gleaming. "What have you done to him, that he has shaved his head and is practicing with your recruits?" she cried.

The doctor had stopped as well, and he made an impatient gesture. "The operating room is reserved for us. We are doing a direct transfer from you to the prince, rather than freezing some of the bone marrow as is sometimes done. He is not doing well, and every moment could make a difference. Can you wait to discuss this until after the procedure?"

The Master slid the phone into his pocket. He held Sophie's gaze. "We will talk later. All will be revealed."

Sophie huffed out a breath. *There was no real choice.* She had made her decision as soon as she heard about the prince, let alone before she saw his pathetic little face. "I expect you to honor your word," she told the Master.

"All will be revealed," the man repeated. Sophie rolled her eyes, and turned to follow the doctor.

CHAPTER FORTY-ONE

Day Thirty-Five

SOPHIE STRETCHED FORWARD to toggle a switch on the dashboard of Connor's speedboat, and emitted a little moan as bruising from the site of the bone marrow harvest reminded her of the procedure. She checked her onboard GPS and programmed in Phi Ni as her destination. She was grateful the boat had started up easily, once she added fuel to the tank. She then paid off the fisherman who'd driven her out to the boat's hidden berth on the atoll.

She set the autopilot and sat back, sipping tea from a thermos and enjoying the wide-open sea, the clouds scudding overhead, the leap of porpoises at the bow.

She'd had time to read the Chris-Craft's operations manual more thoroughly while spending a day post-op, recovering in a hotel paid for by the royal family. She'd been under general anesthesia during the extraction, so she hadn't felt a thing when several holes were made in the back of her hip bone, and a couple of pints of red blood cells, stem cells, and bone marrow liquid removed—leaving her weak the first day, but steadily recovering.

Sophie was still tired, but she didn't want to be away from her baby even a day longer. She expressed the milk she'd produced that wasn't usable due to the anesthesia medication pumped into her for the extraction.

But all of it was worth it when she heard the procedure had gone well for the prince.

Malee, Armita, and Momi had already flown out to Phi Ni on a private charter, after verifying with Nam that no one had come onto the island or made contact. Sophie felt safe using the island as a brief pitstop before returning to Hawaii. So far, there had been no indication that the Yām Khûmkạn knew about Connor's secret holding.

And as long as the Master didn't know what had happened to her mother, he would have no reason to harm her or those close to her by striking at them on Phi Ni.

Sophie tried not to think of Jake, but that was impossible. After a while, she just stopped trying and let the tears rain down and dry on her cheeks in the wind whipping off the ocean.

Sophie piloted the speedboat into the boathouse, in the light of a waning sunset, and tied it up at the wharf. She heard the rumble of a vehicle arriving to pick her up, and felt a lift in her heavy spirits —*she would be seeing her baby soon.*

Alika was driving the work truck that had come down to meet her at the boathouse. Sophie grinned at the sight of his huge smile. She hurried over to hug him with the last of her energy. "I am so glad to see you! How is our baby?"

"She's awesome! Doing great with a new formula, and both her grandma and great-grandma, as well as her aunt and your nanny, fussing over her," Alika said. "Thank you so much for getting her back. You're my hero." He kissed her, a warm buss of friendship, shared history and family, and Sophie let it be what it was.

They got into the truck and drove down the winding, coral stone road through the jungle. Alika gestured to the defunct coconut grove. "This is quite a place Hamilton has."

"Yes, it is. He usually runs the company from here." An idea was taking root in Sophie's mind: she could help Connor run things from

Phi Ni, and stay in her apartment or at her father's on Oahu part-time, and on Kaua'i the rest. The Big Island was off her personal map of destinations for the time being. "What have you been thinking? About how to share time with Momi?"

Alika laughed. "I thought you'd want to rest, relax, get some food, and snuggle with our girl. Trust you to dive right into this tricky topic with both feet." He blew out a breath. "I have a guest house on my property—right now it's rented, but I can kick the guy out. He's one of my workers, just crashing there for a job. I propose that you live with me on Kaua'i for Momi's first year—you can stay out there and have privacy, and I can see Momi as much as I want to during this key time in her life." He squeezed the steering wheel, the knuckles of his remaining hand whitening and darkening with changing pressure. "I know it's an imposition and that you have a job —but the place is wired for high-speed internet. We'd also have built-in babysitting with all the relatives who can't wait to get their hands on Momi, so you could come and go as you need to for work. You can have the cottage at no cost, and access to everything in my house. *Mi casa es su casa,* as they say. And I have a great home gym." He flashed a grin, his dimples as engaging as ever. "Tell me you'll think about it."

"I like that idea." Sophie turned to look fully at Alika. "I can't promise a whole year, though. I will need to go to Oahu, and possibly return to Phi Ni, too. But as a start, for the next few months, your cottage sounds perfect."

Alika grinned in relief. "You've made my day."

She chuckled. "I won't be coming alone, though. Armita will be living with me, and providing the bulk of child care as I need it if you're not available. After Momi's weaned, and we work out how much you have her, Armita could still be available. Consistency is important with young children, and I trust her totally."

"Listen to you—'consistency is important with young children.' You've been studying up, I can tell. We have plenty of time to work out the details." Alika propped his prosthetic hand on the steering wheel to steady it, then patted her leg. "I'm psyched. I'll call home and kick my worker out tomorrow."

Sophie laughed. "Both hands on the steering wheel, please. Only one of those is actually doing anything."

"You mocking Captain Hook here?" Alika held up the plastic prosthetic and waggled it.

"Maybe you should get an actual hook. The men at the gym would love it."

"I'm holding out for a fancy electronic prosthetic, actually." He glanced at Sophie and their eyes met. "If you and Jake get back together, there's room in the cottage for all of you to have your own space."

Sophie looked out the window, blinking. "That won't be happening."

He patted her leg again. "I'm sorry, Sophie."

"Yes. I'm sorry as well." Sophie bit her lip. Her life was plenty full—but it still felt empty without Jake.

CHAPTER FORTY-TWO

Day Thirty-Six

MORNING CAST sharp shadows over the practice field as Connor engaged with Nine in hand-to-hand using staffs. He'd always worked out a lot as a part of his daily routine, but with all of the hours of daily combat practice using every kind of weapon, he could see and feel his body reshaping into something harder, faster, and deadlier.

Nine froze suddenly, lowering his weapon and dropping into the Yām Khûmkạn resting attentive pose, protocol when someone of a higher rank had entered the area. Connor almost struck him, pulling back at the last minute. He spun away and dropped into the same upright position beside Nine, arms at his sides, head up.

Their division leader addressed Connor. "Your presence is required. Come with me."

Connor dropped his staff and followed the man, pulling the loose hood of his robe up to cover his shaved head, as was protocol when off the field. They made their way through the complex and up the stone stairs to the Master's apartments. The leader left Connor at the Master's closed door.

"Enter," the Master's voice said in Thai. Connor had not yet knocked.

Connor stepped inside the sumptuous room. "You sent for me, Master?" *A line out of a B grade movie, but he was living it.*

The Master entered the seating area from the bedroom. He held up a satellite phone. "It is time for you to call Sophie. She has fulfilled her part of the bargain and successfully completed the bone marrow transfer."

"Is she all right?" Connor wiped an arm over his sweaty forehead. His former life had begun to feel like a dream. It wasn't that he didn't think of his dog, his island, his company, his violin—and Sophie. He did—but his days were too full for dwelling on his past. Night, and his dreams, were when those former things haunted him.

"Sophie is perfectly fine. The procedure is painless for the donor. There are residual aches and weakness after, but the body soon rebuilds the lost fluids. The transfer was seamless, and the prince is doing well also." The Master tapped a computer tablet he held. "I have been monitoring Sophie. As soon as she left the hospital, she took a day of rest at a hotel, and then traveled to the coast."

Connor kept his face expressionless. He had not given up the location of his island, and the Master had not asked. *That didn't mean the Master didn't know about it.*

Every night, after dinner, they played chess and engaged in long discussions about politics, economics, science, and justice. Connor learned something new every day, and he couldn't regret the bargain he'd made—*a return to tutelage, in exchange for Sophie's happiness with Jake.* "May I have privacy for this call?"

The Master's inscrutable purple irises bored into him. "Yes. As long as you acknowledge that, by leaving you alone, I am trusting you."

There were many ways to conceal surveillance, and Connor knew them all. The Master could even have the phone set to record the conversation. But he nodded his head, compliant. "Thank you for your trust, Master."

The Master walked out of the room, and shut the door.

Connor took a moment to gather his emotional resistance to Sophie, to ground himself in resolve. He looked around the Master's luxurious chamber, with its wall hangings, carpeting, and ornate carved furniture. He approved of the aesthetic; the beautiful trappings balanced the harsh, ancient stone the rooms were built of. He took a seat in his favorite spot in front of the chessboard near the fireplace.

Sophie's number was saved under the Master's "Favorites," which made him smile.

The phone had a data feature, and Connor took a moment to download the encrypted software he could use to communicate confidentially with Sophie via video feed. Once he had that set up, he scrolled to her number, and hit Contact.

Sophie's face appeared on the tiny screen almost immediately. Connor wanted to smile, but the sight of her, holding Momi's dark curly head tucked beneath her chin, completely choked him up. He cleared his throat, unable to speak. *Damn, but they were beautiful.*

"Connor! It is so good to see you!" Sophie was grinning big enough for both of them. "I just reached out to the Master and insisted that he begin the process of getting you out of there. I didn't expect to hear from you quite so soon!"

"Show me that baby."

Connor felt his heart squeeze as Sophie moved the phone so that it captured Momi's sleeping face. The infant's rosebud mouth was ajar, her cheeks peachy pink, and a welter of soft black curls haloed her head. Sophie stroked her daughter's hair. "I wish you were here so you could hold her, but you'll be here soon. What's the plan to get you out of there? I have the CIA on standby, ready to provide transport."

"I won't ask what deal you made to get them on board," Connor said.

Sophie grimaced. "I've basically promised to become a confidential informant/and or double agent for them. They picked up Jake on the road outside of the compound not long after he was released. I've been working with them ever since."

"How is Jake? Is he recovered?" Connor's pulse pounded uncomfortably. *Jake had recognized him.* Clearly, the man's world was rocked—and he'd jumped to all the right conclusions. It was likely he and Sophie had a lot to talk about. "I hope he had no lasting ill effects."

"Jake's fine. Already back on the Big Island, working."

Did he imagine a tightness around Sophie's lips? Evasiveness in her lowered gaze? She went on. "Let's stay focused. I just want to know where and when to send the CIA to pick you up on the road, or if the Master would like to make some other arrangement."

"I'm not leaving, Sophie." Connor stared into the camera, willing her to look up. At last, she did. Even in the grainy feed, he could see the ashen tone of her skin, a sure sign of distress.

"What do you mean you're not leaving? The Master has to let you go. We had a bargain." The baby squeaked as Sophie squeezed her too tightly.

"I am choosing to stay." Connor threw back the hood that concealed his head, and turned it so that she could see the Thai number tattooed on the back of his shaved scalp. He didn't yet know what that number was—he wouldn't, until he had earned it. "I have agreed to study under the Master."

"No! We have a company for you to run. You can't stay there!" She joggled the baby, who, sensing her mother's upset, let out a cry like an angry kitten.

"I can, and I am. I am choosing to learn from the Master. He's much more knowledgeable and sophisticated than first meets the eye." How could he describe the feats he'd seen the Master do? They sounded like fiction. "I want to stay."

"What are you doing? Becoming a member of the Yām Khûmkạn?" Momi's mewing cries rose in volume. Sophie patted the baby's back vigorously and moved back and forth, in and out of the window of the camera.

"I'm not a member—but I have to go through their program to reach the outcomes I want. I have voluntarily submitted myself to him. It's hard to explain, but he has things to teach me. Powerful things."

"I'm not surprised by anything about that man. I've met him." Sophie shook her head. "He's done something to you. Brainwashed you. Maybe you made some kind of a deal with him?"

Connor raised his hands so that they were visible on the screen. "I swear. I am choosing this." *And he had.* He had chosen to stay and study with the Master, to exchange information with him about their mutual missions. He had done that so that Jake, Sophie and Momi could be a family unit—*and so he didn't have to watch that happen from the outside.*

He had his own destiny to forge. And maybe, someday, looking at Sophie and her baby wouldn't hurt so much.

Connor gasped in surprise as Sophie abruptly pulled down the scoop neck of her shirt and guided the squalling baby to her breast. Momi calmed instantly. Sophie closed her eyes, clearly relaxing into something mysterious and beautiful, a connection he'd never have or experience.

A long moment went by before Connor could tear his eyes away. "I have to go. I have meditation practice."

"This is ridiculous. You can't do this!" Sophie cried, her serenity disappearing. "The company needs you!"

"No, the company needs *you.*" He kept his eyes averted—watching her nurse the baby was wreaking havoc on his body. "If you wake up my computer, and log in with the password I'm going to send you, you'll find a signed and notarized document dated a year ago, designating you as my heir, and/or my power of attorney in any absence. I have thought long and hard about who I would leave my world to, and you were the only one. There was only ever you, Sophie."

Better not to engage with her in a fruitless argument and upset the baby again.

Better to say goodbye now.

Better just to end the call.

Feeling like he was cutting off his own arm, Connor punched the button and bowed forward, curling over in a white-hot ball of pain around the phone in his fist. Would he ever see her again? Would it ever stop hurting if he did?

"You have made the right decision," The Master said from the doorway. "Come. It's time for meditation class. I have a new lesson for you and the students."

Connor got up and handed the Master the phone. "Thank you for letting me speak privately."

The Master turned off the phone, already buzzing like an angry insect with Sophie's attempted callback. "You can leave whenever you feel satisfied with achieving the life you are longing for."

"And that is what you understand, that she does not," Connor said. "It's too hard to watch her with someone else. I need my own life."

The Master inclined his head. "And you shall have it." He turned on his heel.

Connor followed him—and with every step he took, he felt lighter.

CHAPTER FORTY-THREE

Day Thirty-Six

Sᴏᴘʜɪᴇ ᴄᴀʀʀɪᴇᴅ a fed and sleeping Momi back to the bassinet that Nam's wife had procured for her. She lay the baby down, and notified Armita on the baby monitor that she was going to the computer lab for a few hours. "Let me know if she needs anything that you can't figure out."

Armita snorted, and then appeared in the doorway carrying a basket of peas as well as the monitor. She sat on the rocking chair beside the bassinet. "I will watch over her from here."

"You don't have to. The house is full of people ready to respond to her littlest cry." Sophie was glad Alika's *tutu* and mother had at last been persuaded to go for a walk to pick up shells on the island's deserted beaches.

"Momi will be watched over every minute of every day. We will not lose her again," Armita said. "But after the peas are prepared, I might take a little nap, as well."

"You do that." Sophie's gaze fell to the bedside table. Jake's ring, and the envelope it was placed on, still rested there. She walked over and picked up both items, turning on her heel to leave the room without any explanation. Sophie loved that Armita never asked any questions that Sophie did not welcome. She simply accepted.

Sophie headed out of her bedroom, down the open hallway, and across the inner courtyard to Connor's office.

Her mind was still whirling from the things he'd told her. How long would he be gone? What had the Master done to persuade him to stay? Could she send a team to extract him?

She already knew the answer to that one—the fortress was nearly impregnable, and the United States had no interest in poking that hornets' nest. Even Security Solutions didn't have enough men with a death wish to take it on.

The office's cool, gray walls calmed her immediately with the familiar environment of a distraction-free computer lab. Sophie lowered the blinds that opened into the central courtyard and the trickling Quan Yin fountain.

Her muscles were knotted and her throat tight from the talk with Connor. Working out would help. Sophie walked over to his Bowflex set and sat down on the bench. She adjusted the settings, and began lat pulldowns—she needed to strengthen her upper body with all the baby carrying she was doing.

Of all the things she had braced herself for, Connor's refusal to return was not one of them.

He must be brainwashed by the Master, or perhaps the man had found some leverage on him that Sophie didn't know about. But Connor had not seemed under duress; she knew his body language, his every expression, the inflections of his voice. Though most of what he showed the world was a mask—*she alone really knew him.*

Sophie fought tears for the second time that day and coughed, her throat still tight. She looked around for water—now that she was breastfeeding, she was constantly thirsty. She filled a paper cup of water from the dispenser in the corner, sipping it and composing herself.

She was glad she had been able to see his very real pain at saying goodbye—and also the determination in his mouth, the hard line of his jaw.

Whatever was going on, Connor meant it. And he was quite motivated, if his shaved and tattooed head were anything to judge by. It didn't matter. She'd find a way to get him out.

But first, she needed to pull back. Retrench. Recover from all that had happened. Pick up the reins of the company, and keep it going. Notify the families of the men who'd died on the mission, and help bury the dead. And in the meantime, work with the CIA on all of this, including the situation with her mother.

Sophie went back to the workout area and completed a vigorous forty minutes of exercise, drank more water, and sat down in Connor's ergonomic office chair. She woke up his computer and logged in with the access code he had texted her over their secure line.

The computer immediately opened up to a saved file, and Sophie recognized a copy of the letter Connor had written her when he and Jake first marooned her on the island.

She whisked the letter aside. She could not bear to read it again right now.

The signed will and power of attorney were all in order. She opened an email and sent them to Kendall Bix, President of Operations, along with a request for a video conference meeting with all the department heads of Security Solutions. They deserved to get this news through videoconferencing, at least.

He had asked her to run the company, so run it she would. She'd keep it going for him to come back to.

She opened another file. This one was filled with accounts and passwords; all of Connor's secret money stashes around the world.

She could help herself to billions—but she couldn't care less about that. Money had always been a given in her life, and the salary and stock options he'd set up for her were more than generous.

The small skull that represented the Ghost software, Connor's vigilante justice program, pulsed at her. A tiny icon showed a number of situations that needed attention.

But she hadn't promised to keep the Ghost going for him, too. She wasn't comfortable with his chosen mission; she never had been, though with time she'd come to see and appreciate the utility of it. *But right now?* "That's one can of worms you don't need to open, girlfriend," Marcella's voice said in her mind.

She minimized the Ghost icon and it blipped out of view. She powered down the computer, and her eyes dropped to take in Jake's letter in its sealed envelope, held down by the black velvet ring box.

He'd said the ring was an antique. The corners of the little black box were worn, the velvet rubbed off, testifying to age and sentiment.

She opened a drawer and uncovered a bubble-wrapped envelope. She addressed it to Jake on the Big Island, and slid the box in. It seemed wrong to just throw it in there with no word, so she scribbled on a Post-it: *"I wish you every happiness."* She stuck it in with the ring and sealed the envelope before she could change her mind. Nam would know how to get the ring into the mail and insure it.

Jake was a hero. A good man. He deserved to be happy, and she wouldn't make him happy. She'd always known that, but had hoped, for a little while . . .

Sophie pulled a handful of tissues out of a nearby box and blew her nose. Dabbed her eyes. Got up and drank more water. *"Son of a two-headed goat.* All this crying. Does nothing! Changes nothing. Useless emotions!"

The soundproofed room didn't give her back so much as an echo.

She picked up the letter. *He had asked her to destroy it without reading it.*

Some part of her had always known that Jake needed to be the only man in her life. With Alika as the father of her child and Connor as someone she would always love more than a friend, he had hit a wall. She understood that.

Her fingers played with the edge of the envelope's flap. Oh, how she missed Jake's comforting presence, his strong arms, the rumble of his voice in her ear, teasing her. She longed to read his loving words, to feel the incredible feelings he stirred in her one more time. To have been loved the way he'd loved her—*what a gift.*

But was that what she missed most? How he'd loved her? Or did she miss the man, himself?

She didn't know the answer, and trying to think about it was making her physically sick. It wasn't fair to either of them for her to read whatever was written in this letter. She reached under the desk, pulled the shredder forward, and fed the letter in, her vision blurring.

EPILOGUE

Six months later

SOPHIE SLID her key into the door of Connor's apartment at the swanky Pendragon Arches building on Oahu. She glanced around out of habit, checking the familiar hallway for danger. Nothing visible but immaculate carpet and spotlighted artworks. The refined surroundings she'd first approached years ago had become familiar in the month she'd been living there, but when she opened the door, a completely new and refurbished interior greeted her.

Anubis, his ears pricked, sat on his haunches. He whined happily at the sight of her, his intelligent eyes bright. She still missed Ginger's sloppy, rambunctious affection, but as she and Jake had agreed, Ginger and Tank remained together and lived with him on the Big Island.

"Hey boy." She patted the Doberman's sleek head and caressed his ears. "Keep a good eye on my girl and Armita today?"

The dog gave a snort, as if to chide her for even asking such a thing.

Armita came out from the bedroom area carrying Momi. The baby reached her arms eagerly for Sophie and grinned, showing off three shiny new teeth. She burbled something that might have been *"Mama!"*

Sophie's heart broke into a thousand pieces. "Darling girl!" She embraced Armita and Momi both. "Eight hours feels like forever being away from you."

Armita stepped back, still holding Momi. "Our girl has something new to demonstrate, Sophie Malee."

"What is it? Show me!" It seemed as if every day, Momi met some new milestone.

Armita set the baby down on the immaculate, camel-colored carpeting Sophie had chosen to replace the flooring that had been destroyed in an explosion in the apartment's previous incarnation. The baby, set on all fours, rocked back-and-forth, concentrating. Anubis sat down in front of Momi, giving an encouraging *"Woof."*

Momi fastened her gaze on the dog and extended a hand, fingers spread, and shuffled forward on her knees. She did it again on the other side. Anubis moved back, staying just out of reach, and she chortled, speeding up.

"She's crawling!" Sophie exclaimed. She elbowed Anubis aside and dropped to her knees in front of the baby. "Come to Mama, my pearl."

Momi giggled, a sound that Sophie knew would be tattooed on her heart forever, and she crawled right up into Sophie's lap.

Sophie scooped her close. She tickled the baby's tummy and blew on her neck, and those wonderful giggles filled the whole room.

Was there any love as overwhelming as the love of a mother? The incredible feelings Momi brought up on a daily basis reminded Sophie of her own mother.

Pim Wat had survived her fall, and remained captive in Guantánamo. A picture of her that McDonald had sent during their call that day showed that the broken bones in Pim Wat's face had not been skillfully set. Her hair had gone white, seemingly overnight, and she had lost an alarming amount of weight as she sank into a catatonic state.

Pim Wat's beauty was gone, and her deep depression appeared genuine.

McDonald was very disappointed. "Haven't got a whisper of usable intel out of her," he told Sophie on their conference call. "She just lies there, completely unresponsive. Even after we gave her electroshock therapy for her depression." He grinned, and it was more than a little evil.

"Don't underestimate her. She can never be allowed to escape." Sophie knew exactly what her mother looked like in that state—and Sophie'd been afraid, at one time, that she might end up in a similar bad way.

"Don't worry. She's not going anywhere. But I'm thinking it's about time for you to reach out to the Master. Check on your man in the compound."

"He's not my man."

"Whatever you need to tell yourself. But reach out. See if you can get a dialogue going with the Master, or with Hamilton. We still want to know more of what the Yām Khûmkạn is up to, and we're getting nothing from Pim Wat."

The CIA had leaked that they had captured Pim Wat on her way to visit her sister in Bangkok, in order to deflect the Master's attention from Malee and Sophie. Sophie assumed that the Master had picked up that intel, as the CIA had intentionally disseminated it. There had been no response from the Yām Khûmkạn and no further communication from the stronghold.

Armita brought Sophie back to the present moment, waving a spoon from the kitchen area. "There's time for you to take Anubis and the baby out for your evening run before dinner," she said. "I have a nice coconut curry for us when you get home."

"What have I done to deserve you?" Sophie stood up with the baby in her arms and gave Armita a kiss on the cheek. "You keep me sane. You keep everything going. You make it so that I can go to work every day and not worry about Momi, or anything going on at home."

Armita's cheeks flushed. "It's my pleasure," the Thai woman said with dignity. "Now get going before the rice clumps up too much." She turned back to the stove.

Momi reached up and grabbed Sophie's abundant hair, giving a tug at her curly locks and emitting an enthusiastic squeal. "You understood Auntie Armita, didn't you, darling? Okay, let's go."

Sophie bundled the baby into her high-end jogging stroller and put Anubis on his harness. The Doberman was incredibly well-behaved, which was a relief when she imagined trying to manage Ginger, and a stroller, and all the traffic of Honolulu's busy sidewalks. Maybe God knew that the time just wasn't right for Sophie to have a dog as challenging to manage as Ginger had always been. Just as important, she knew that Ginger was happy with Tank and Jake, and that eased her mind, too.

They got on the elevator and were soon out on the sidewalk. Anubis always drew attention with his sleek and regal bearing, and the hint of danger that surrounded his watchful eyes and cocked ears. He was an excellent guardian as well as companion—perfect for her new life.

Honolulu was winding down for the day. Commuter traffic was brisk, and families were out walking their dogs, jogging and riding bikes in the balmy evening. Sophie trotted along the sidewalk pushing the stroller with Anubis beside her, enjoying the sights and sounds as they headed for Ala Moana Beach Park.

Momi spotted one of the hot dog vendors who also sold balloons. She shrieked with excitement, waving her chubby arms at the sight of the brightly colored spheres. Sophie steered the stroller over to the hot dog wagon. Anubis, smelling one of his favorite treats, emitted a tiny whine, the only indication she would get from him about what he wanted.

"I think both of you deserve a treat." She bought a hot dog and fed the meat to Anubis, and then she bought a bright yellow balloon and tied it to the stroller's surround.

Momi yelled with glee, grabbing at the ribbon holding the

balloon and batting it with her hands. They resumed their gentle jog toward the ocean.

Once they reached the beach, Sophie gave Anubis the hand signal to sit and stay, and parked the big-wheeled jogging stroller on the sand. She lifted the baby out, and Momi kicked her legs with excitement as Sophie set her in the sand on her little padded bottom.

Momi promptly grabbed a handful of sand, and it headed toward her mouth.

"No, darling. Not for eating," Sophie said, peeling the baby's fingers open to let the sand out. Momi squawked in protest, but then spotted an abandoned red plastic shovel a few feet away. She engaged her new skill of crawling to head toward it.

Sophie sighed. The baby had been so frustrated with wanting things and not being able to get to them in the last month—and now she could, and that brought new challenges. Every time Sophie turned around, it seemed like her daughter had grown exponentially. Her life was too full for her to dwell on much but keeping up with it all—and still, late at night, she woke feeling the emptiness of the bed beside her.

The sun, lowering towards the horizon, cast golden beams across them as they enjoyed the day's heat trapped in the sand. Sophie's gaze wandered out over the ocean, and as she watched her baby, she couldn't help thinking of Jake. He'd enjoy seeing the gusto with which Momi embraced every new experience—that was how Jake lived, too.

Jake had left Security Solutions and moved to Kona, where he'd started his own private investigation company. Felicia had gone with him, and Sophie suspected they were living together. With no one available to staff it, Sophie had made the tough executive decision to close the Big Island office. Truth was, she had always suspected that Connor had just opened that extension so that she and Jake would have something to do-over there.

Alika's business was thriving on Kaua'i; she had spent a wonderful five months in his guest house, getting her feet under her as a parent and learning the ropes of running Security Solutions virtually, with just a few board and planning meetings she'd flown to Oahu for. Eventually, there had come a point when she needed to step up fully as head of the company, and now she went into the corporate building every day and occupied Connor's very comfortable office.

She was just keeping his chair warm for him.

The camera Rhinehart had installed over the Yām Khûmkạn stronghold doorway had a one-year battery. Every so often, late at night when the baby and Armita were in bed, Sophie logged into the live stream feed channeled through the Security Solutions tablet that had been recovered by the CIA from the gravesite in the jungle.

She'd traded information about some of Connor's Ghost cases to McDonald to get access to that video stream, and she didn't regret it —because, once in a while, she would see Connor's form, taller than the rest of the recruits, moving about in the dining hall where the camera was aimed. Sometimes he'd be seated at one of the long wooden tables, eating a simple meal of beans, rice, and vegetables with the other trainees. She could always pick him out by his build and pale skin, and she looked for any signs of distress.

There were none.

Connor laughed with the other men. She saw his mouth moving, his hands gesturing, his ready smile. Whatever had led to the decision to stay at the stronghold, he clearly wasn't suffering. She had to assume that he hadn't been coerced, that he'd truly wanted to stay. So, for now, she was content just to check in on him when she could.

Sophie packed up the baby, cleaning off the sand as best she could, and they headed back in the blue shadows of a warm Honolulu evening. At the Pendragon Arches building, Sophie tried once again to get the sand off the baby's skin and out of Anubis's paws before going through the grand lobby with its old-world charm and chandeliers.

Of the many places that had been available for her and her little party to stay in, she had most wanted something that said "do over," as her mother had asked for so many months ago. Her old Mary Watson place was too small for her current needs, and so was her father's place, especially now that he had officially retired and occupied it. The company apartment had made sense, and she had supervised its renovation from Kaua`i.

Delicious smells greeted them as Sophie unlocked the door again, stepping inside and handing the baby to Armita so that she could deal with the stroller and the dog's harness—and she never forgot to engage the door's security measures.

"My goodness, Momi, all of this sand!" Armita told the baby. She said that every night when they returned, with fond indulgence in her voice. Armita loved bathing Momi, so Sophie didn't comment as the nanny carried the baby off to the bathroom to be rinsed, changed and dressed.

Sophie took that time to strip out of her clothing and take a quick shower herself, reveling in a few moments alone.

Within the hour, the three of them were seated at the little dining room table, and Momi was slinging handfuls of rice at them with startling accuracy.

"I have a little extra work to do tonight," Sophie told Armita as she cleaned up Momi's mess after the meal. "I'm going next door."

Next door.

Next door was the other reason Sophie had chosen this apartment over any other. The Ghost had conducted his activities in a secret office in the apartment next to his living quarters. The setup inside was just the same as when Sophie and Connor had worked there together so long ago. Connor's calm, cool computer lab had missed being damaged in the bomb blast that wrecked Sophie's current abode.

Armita nodded. "I'll keep watch in case Momi wakes up."

Sophie nursed the baby and put her down. Once Momi was asleep in her bassinet beside Sophie's bed, Sophie walked to the bedroom closet and opened the door.

Sophie's shoes and clothing took up little space in the walk-in—

she was a wardrobe minimalist. As she faced the floor-to-ceiling shoe rack at the back of the closet, Sophie remembered the first time she had discovered the entrance to Connor's secret world. She never would have dreamed that, a few short years later, she would be pressing a lever that moved the shoe rack out of the way, and stepping through a hidden door into the Ghost's computer cockpit.

That cool, secret space, humming with technology, was hers now.

Turn the page for a sneak peek of, *Wired Truth*, Paradise Crime Thrillers book 10.

SNEAK PEEK

WIRED TRUTH, PARADISE CRIME THRILLERS BOOK 10

Two years after Wired Courage
Sophie: Day One

"DIAMONDS ARE NOT FOREVER." Henry Childer, manager of Finewell's Auction House Honolulu, had a damp handclasp and a plummy British accent. "My diamonds are gone, and I need them found by next week."

Sophie Smithson gestured to the seating area in front of her desk, and wiped her hand on her narrow black pants, out of his view. "Please have a seat, Mr. Childer, and you can tell me all about it. You've come to the right place—Security Solutions specializes in confidential investigations. I have some documents for you to sign that will clarify things. You can review them while I fix us some tea."

Childer looked her over as he took a seat, clearly surprised at her accent. "Delightful to encounter a fellow countryman in this place, and a cup of tea as well, Ms. Smithson." He tugged a handkerchief from his front pocket and mopped his shiny forehead, pale eyes blinking rapidly. "Infernal Hawaii heat. I don't know how you stand it."

Sophie set a computer tablet, already loaded with the company's intake forms and disclosures, at the man's elbow. "Actually, I'm American and Thai, but educated in Europe." She walked over to a glossy wood credenza and pushed a button. A coffee and tea service, along with the equipment for preparation, rose from within. Paula, her assistant, cleaned and stocked it daily, and all Sophie had to do was press a button to begin the water heating. "Do you take lemon or milk in your tea?"

"Milk and two sugars, please. Anything can be endured with a spot of tea, they say, but I'm afraid this is a most distressing situation."

"You said diamonds are missing?" Sophie assembled the tea things on a tray.

"I'm manager of the Honolulu branch of Finewell's Auction House, as I told you. Are you familiar with our company? We're the premier auction house for luxury collectibles in the Western Hemisphere."

That was a big claim to make, but Sophie nodded politely. "Please elaborate on how you came to have the diamonds, and what you know about their disappearance."

"The stones are part of a family-owned set that is being auctioned off next weekend. They arrived at our vault and were authenticated upon arrival—all part of our protocol. We cannot vouch for something that is not truthfully represented."

Once she had their cups prepared, Sophie arranged them on a tray and returned, setting the beverages down on the low table in front of the couch where Childer sat. She took a sleek modern armchair across from him and propped her own computer tablet on her knee, tapping to wake it up. She dosed her dark Thai tea with honey, and began inputting details for his case into a new file.

"This appears to be in order." Childer stashed a pair of reading glasses in his breast pocket, and handed her back the intake information. Sophie scanned the forms as he lifted his teacup. He pursed pink lips and blew upon his tea, then took a sip. "Excellent, my dear.

The set was received, verified as authentic, and stored in our secure vault. All was in order at that time; I watched a video of that process and signed off on it per usual."

Sophie held up a hand. "I see, from this application, that you are hiring Security Solutions yourself. Not as a representative of Finewell's."

"Correct." Childer's cup rattled in its saucer as he set it down.

"I see. Please, go on."

"It's part of my role to oversee preparing the items for sale—photographing them for the publicity catalogs and whatnot. I went to the vault to pull the set for the photographer, and it was gone. I was most perturbed, but had the presence of mind to reschedule the photography shoot. I verified that the other items for that weekend's auction were all accounted for. Only the diamonds had disappeared; the parure included a necklace, earrings, a ring, a bracelet, and even a hair clip. Assessed value was three million dollars."

Sophie blinked at the cost. "Why didn't you notify the police?"

"A theft from our supposedly secure location would be a great scandal. Terrible for the company, and catastrophic for me personally. That's why I'm here on my own dime, as the Americans say." Childer dabbed his mouth with a paper napkin. "I will, of course, disclose the theft if we are not able to reclaim the jewels by next Friday."

"The sale is next Saturday, you said?" Sophie frowned. "Today is Thursday. Eight days is not long to find something like this. That's cutting it close."

"All I can ask is that you try." Childer reached into the inside pocket of his suit jacket and removed a checkbook. "What do you require for a deposit?"

After the contracts were signed and funds exchanged, Childer pointed a plump finger at Sophie. "I researched whom to approach. I want *you* to work on this for me. I can't have this case given to someone who won't treat it with the sensitivity it deserves."

"Mr. Childer." Sophie set her tablet down. "I appreciate your confidence in me, but I'm CEO of Security Solutions. I no longer personally handle cases."

"Please." Childer placed his hands palm-to-palm and bowed a little in her direction. "I looked for the best private investigators and company available, and was delighted to find Security Solutions right here in Honolulu. I was even more impressed with you personally." He ticked off her accomplishments on his fingers. "A trained ex-FBI agent with a background in tech. Inventor of the Data Analysis Victim Information Database crime solving software, and CEO of the top-ranked security company in the United States with a seventy-five percent case closure rate." He gave her a frank once-over. "And a goddess in the flesh who makes a lovely cup of tea."

Sophie smiled at the praise, and ducked her head. "That last part has little actual application to crime solving. I will have to run this by Kendall Bix, our President of Operations. He is in charge of case assignments."

"But you'll consider it? Tell me you will."

"I'll consider it. You've caught me at a vulnerable moment, Mr. Childer. I've been up to my eyebrows in quarterly reports. Who wouldn't rather get into the field, while a clock is ticking, to solve the mystery of a set of missing diamonds?" She stood, smoothing sleek black pants made for movement, and braced herself to shake his damp hand again. "We'll need to come in to review your video footage and see the scene of the crime, as it were. I'll be in touch."

Continue reading *Wired Truth*: tobyneal.net/WTwb

ACKNOWLEDGMENTS

Dear Readers!

I am so excited to complete this latest wild ride with Sophie and her growing family. Thank you for coming with us on this journey!

I have to say that this book was even more intense than many of the others. The characters continue to do what they're going to do, and it's downright hard to herd them towards the happy ending that I envisioned originally. That said, you know my storylines and that I always want three things to happen: good to triumph over evil, love to win in the end, and the characters to have experiences that make them grow into better people.

And sometimes, those characters hit a wall. They get to do that, just as we do—and Jake hit that wall in this book. Should we be mad at him for it?

I'm not. I actually think Felicia is a better match for him in the long run—a woman he can truly be happy with. He's made some choices that take him in another direction, and for her part, Sophie has let him go—though not without deeply appreciating how his love has helped and healed her from her past. Every relationship, whether it continues or not, has the potential to help us grow to be better people, and both Sophie and Jake grew through their time together.

The part that gives me the most angst in this whole story (besides the death of Thom Tang!) is Connor's sacrifice for Jake and Sophie to be together—but as the story hints at, he made that choice for himself too. Connor wanted a new challenge, new ways to grow, and the Master is providing that for him.

Sophie is on a journey of self-discovery. That has been the theme of all of these books. She is learning and growing through her work, through her relationships, and now, through motherhood, finding who she really is as a woman in the world. I expect that in the next book, more will be revealed about the Master, Pim Wat, the CIA, and Sophie's own heart. And for the first time in the whole series, Sophie is completely alone to figure that out. She has a lot on her plate as she fully steps into her potential as a woman and a leader.

Momi has brought a new facet into Sophie's life that stabilizes, heals, and gives her a purpose. But Sophie also has other purposes besides motherhood, as do all of us modern women. She has a multi-million-dollar company to run, crimes to solve, and friends to help her in time of need—as well as room in her heart for a special someone. I can't wait to see what she does with Security Solutions, and with the Ghost software, in the future. Will she fully occupy not just Connor's corner office chair, but his alter ego? I look forward, and I hope you do too, to the next installment of her journey in *Wired Truth*, coming in 2019.

Want to know how I get so many crazy ideas? On December 30, 2018, I'm releasing my personal memoir, *Freckled: A Memoir of Growing Up Wild in Hawaii*. I'm very excited to let you know that it is available for preorder under my nonfiction writing name, TW Neal. Check it out on my website HERE. If you read the memoir, you'll get a good notion of where it all started for me, growing up as a hippie kid living in a tent in the jungle, completely off the grid, on the North Shore of Kaua`i in the 1970s.

As always, thanks go out to my awesome helpers: Jamie Davis, Bonnie Hodur, and Don Williams, as well as my faithful typo hunters, Shirley and Angie—each of you are fabulous and important.

It takes a village to write a book, and bring it out into the world, and you are my A-team!

If you enjoyed this book, or the series, would you please leave a review? I so appreciate every single one of them! Just a few words are fine. Mahalo!

Hope you enjoy the sneak peek of *Wired Truth*! And until next time, I'll be writing!

Much aloha,

Toby Neal

P.S. Check out the *Freckled* memoir on my website: tobyneal.net/Frwb

FREE BOOKS

Join my mystery and romance lists and receive free, full-length, award-winning ebooks of *Torch Ginger & Somewhere on St. Thomas* as welcome gifts: tobyneal.net/TNNews

TOBY'S BOOKSHELF

PARADISE CRIME SERIES

Paradise Crime Mysteries
Blood Orchids
Torch Ginger
Black Jasmine
Broken Ferns
Twisted Vine
Shattered Palms
Dark Lava
Fire Beach
Rip Tides
Bone Hook
Red Rain
Bitter Feast
Razor Rocks
Wrong Turn
Shark Cove
Coming 2021

Paradise Crime Mysteries Novella
Clipped Wings

Paradise Crime Mystery
Special Agent Marcella Scott
Stolen in Paradise

Paradise Crime Suspense Mysteries
Unsound

Paradise Crime Thrillers
Wired In
Wired Rogue
Wired Hard
Wired Dark
Wired Dawn
Wired Justice
Wired Secret
Wired Fear
Wired Courage
Wired Truth
Wired Ghost
Wired Strong
Wired Revenge
Coming 2021

ROMANCES
Toby Jane

The Somewhere Series
Somewhere on St. Thomas
Somewhere in the City
Somewhere in California

The Somewhere Series
Secret Billionaire Romance
Somewhere in Wine Country
Somewhere in Montana
Date TBA
Somewhere in San Francisco
Date TBA

A Second Chance Hawaii Romance
Somewhere on Maui

Co-Authored Romance Thrillers
The Scorch Series
Scorch Road
Cinder Road
Smoke Road
Burnt Road
Flame Road
Smolder Road

YOUNG ADULT

Standalone
Island Fire

NONFICTION
TW Neal

Memoir
Freckled
Open Road

ABOUT THE AUTHOR

Kirkus Reviews calls Neal's writing, *"persistently riveting. Masterly."*

Award-winning, USA Today bestselling social worker turned author Toby Neal grew up on the island of Kaua`i in Hawaii. Neal is a mental health therapist, a career that has informed the depth and complexity of the characters in her stories. Neal's mysteries and thrillers explore the crimes and issues of Hawaii from the bottom of the ocean to the top of volcanoes. Fans call her stories, *"Immersive, addicting, and the next best thing to being there."*

Neal also pens romance, romantic thrillers, and writes memoir/non-fiction under TW Neal.

Visit tobyneal.net for more ways to stay in touch!

or

Join my Facebook readers group, *Friends Who Like Toby Neal Books,* for special giveaways and perks.

Made in the USA
Middletown, DE
13 November 2022

14918936R00151